THE BEAUFORT DIARIES

THE BEAUFORT DIARIES

T COOPER

Illustrations by Alex Petrowsky

MELVILLEHOUSE
BROOKLYN, NEW YORK

THE BEAUFORT DIARIES
© 2010 T Cooper

Illustrations © 2010 Alex Petrowsky

First Melville House printing: February 2010

Melville House Publishing
145 Plymouth Street
Brooklyn, NY 11201

www.mhpbooks.com

ISBN: 978-1-935554-07-3

Book design by Kelly Blair

Printed in China

Library of Congress Cataloging-in-Publication Data

Cooper, T.
 The Beaufort diaries / T Cooper ; illustrations by Alex Petrowsky.
   p. cm.
ISBN 978-1-935554-07-3
1. Graphic novels. I. Petrowsky, Alex. II. Title.
PN6727.C638B43 2010
741.5'973--dc22
                                            2009052753

To:
Dixie & Matilda
(but not Allison)

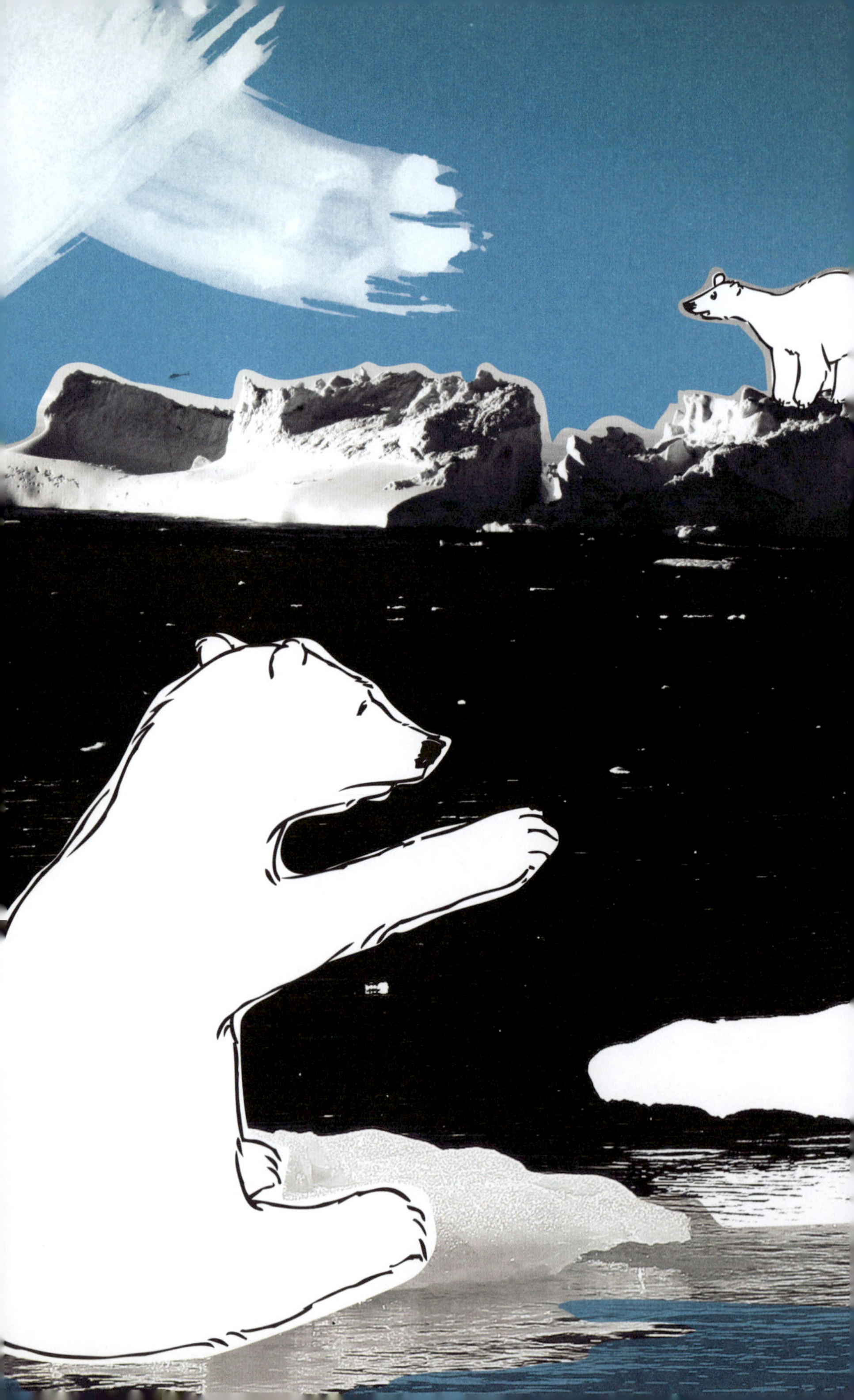

I

If you really want to hear about it, the first thing you'll probably want to know is where I came from and what my parents were like, and all that Inuit legend crap about how some of us shed our skins, walk upright, and become men. But I don't really feel like going into any of that because it's so boring, and if it bores me, then it sure as hell is going to bore you.

What I *will* tell you is that my dad split (*boo-hoo*), and my mom was always rattling on about how it was because times were hard, harder than they'd ever been, *blah blah blah*, and that unlike back in the day, nowadays you couldn't *buy* a ringed seal out there if you wanted to. "The ice is shrinking and the temperature's rising!" She repeated it daily (even though it always seemed cold as an Eskimo's tit to me), so my dad had to travel longer distances to bring home the blubber, and that's why he was gone all the time—to take care of us. *Whatever.* I bought her story then, but looking back, it just sounds like typical mother-making-excuses-for-absentee-father B.S. to me.

But I didn't always feel this way, and it's not where my story begins anyway. It starts with me, adrift on the broken sea ice in the place our family had lived for generations, the south Beaufort Sea. My mother had taken me out on a mission to demonstrate how to sniff out and sneak up on a seal (not that there were that many to be sniffed in the first place), but the next thing I knew, I heard the loudest *CRAAAACK* imaginable, and the ice beneath me started vibrating and shaking, and then a massive chasm gaped open between us, and the ice floe sheared free and started floating away. With me on it.

My mother just stood there watching. I wanted to jump in and paddle back to her, but I was so hungry and tired, and she was getting so far away—I didn't think I could make it. "Ma, why don't you swim to me?" I think I was hollering, but I don't know if anything came out. I could tell she was crying as she grew smaller and smaller and I drifted farther and farther...

Soon she was gone and I was all alone for the first time in my life—the only sound coming from the icy water slapping out a faint drum-beat against the bottom of my floe.

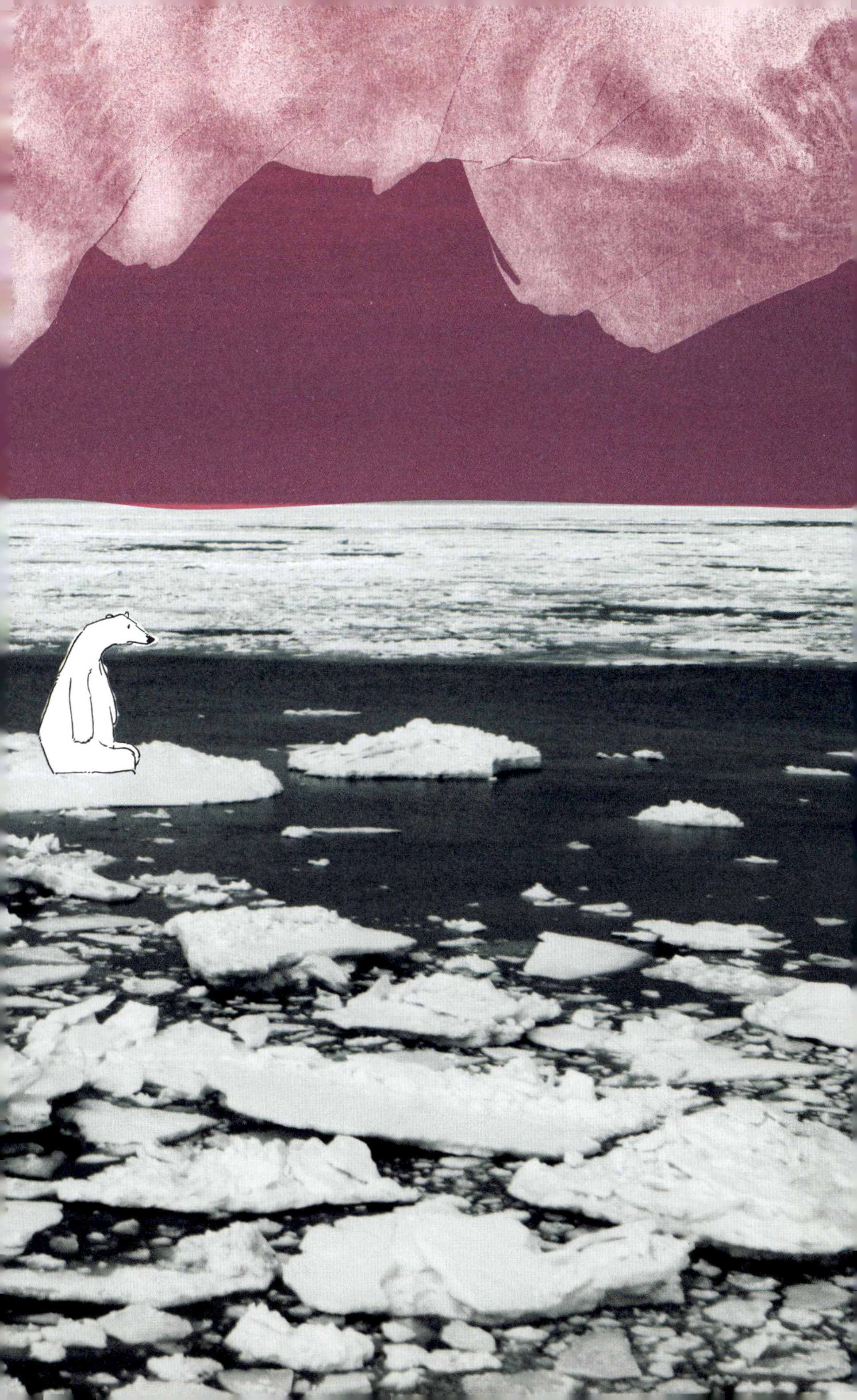

II

Contrary to what certain people want you to think, there is nothing natural for me about eating fish and berries. You don't just "adapt." Face it: fish is *fishy*, and berries, well, they're generally pretty bitter, and they taste like shit. Not to mention they don't fill you up. Nevertheless, when my little chunk of ice landed and jarred me from sleep, I didn't know how long I'd been floating, or where the hell I was. But the first thing I sensed were little berries pelting me from somewhere above, bouncing off my head before settling into purple stains on the ice beside me. One of the blots almost looked to be the shape of my mother. Or maybe it was a witch, I couldn't really decide.

"How about that?" I heard a man's voice say. Other people mumbled to one another and gathered to stare down at me on my floe. And then I realized I had to be in Alaska, because the voice didn't say, "How *aboot* that?" He said, "How *about* that," like regular. So I asked him something like, "Which way is home?" but he just pointed north and laughed, his black brushy mustache twitching under a red nose. A little girl in a yellow raincoat tossed a dead fish down then, and it bounced twice before landing against my fur. I ate it. I had no choice.

Eventually people stopped coming 'round, so I hauled myself onto a splintery wooden dock and attempted a few wobbly steps to steady my ice legs. I was so stiff, my neck killing from the way I'd been sleeping with my head propped against a tiny crag of ice. I stumbled down what seemed to be the main street of town; there were rusty pick-up trucks with rows of shotguns in their gun-racks, a brightly-lit check-cashing joint, and a couple ragtag liquor stores. Captain Patty's Seafood beckoned, and I pressed my nose up against the window to scout out the scene inside. It smelled inviting, but I knew "seafood" didn't mean *seal*-food. I jammed my paws into my fur and turned to go. But *wait*, there was something in there—*What the*? It was a twenty-dollar American bill, rolled up with a string of seaweed. *Ma*?

III

I gobbled the pile of crab legs that Rosie the waitress set in front of me, plus some raw salmon on the side. You know how people stranded in the desert are sometimes reduced to eating sand in their delirium? That's how I thought of fish and crab. Rosie slid me some free seconds and cooed, "You're awful handsome," while scratching the hair on my chin. I had four dollars left after tip.

Back on Main Street, I passed by the window of a sporting goods store, where I spotted a red hunting cap with one of those long bills and ear flaps. It was marked $6.99, but the guy let me have it for $4. I plopped the hat on my head—seemed like the thing to do. I didn't care if it was corny; I thought I looked good when I saw my reflection in a mirror.

Rosie had mentioned an ex-fiancé who'd just been hired on a fish-processing boat that was leaving the next morning for a month at sea. She told me to

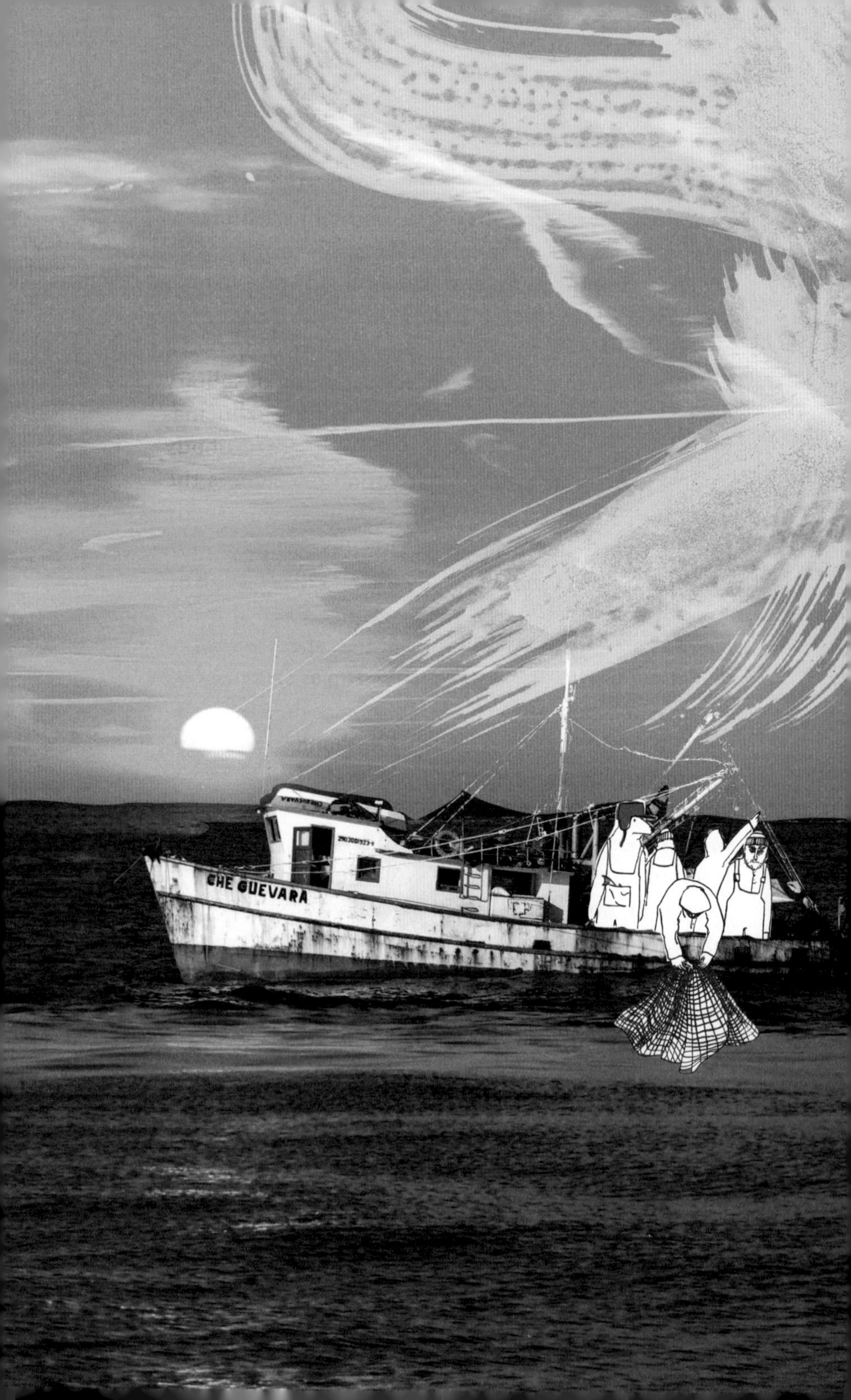
CHE GUEVARA

ask for Joe and I'd get on the rig no problem. So I was hired as a slimer on the line, killing, gutting and sorting the catch. It was the lowliest job on the totem pole (besides chef's helper, but they didn't have a hair-net big enough for me).

Thus began a seemingly endless string of solitary days filled with ten-foot swells and hazy hallucinations of my mother bobbing in the distance. Nobody would talk to me and I was so lonely, but it was the only work I could secure without papers. Eventually I moved onto a harvesting boat and worked my way up to deckhand, pulling in the catch and earning an actual percentage of the crew's share. I saved every paycheck in full—what was there to spend it on?—because I wanted to get out of Alaska as soon as possible. Too much like home.

You could say I grew up quick, thanks to a steady diet of surplus salmon steaks, flat, watery beer by the keg, and the same ten-year-old, dog-eared copies of *Juggs* magazine that got passed around the bunks. Every night I had no choice but to listen as the other guys told nonstop, torrid tales about women, purportedly trying to teach me all I'd ever need to know once I "got up on the horse" myself. (If I never hear another fishy-fingers joke again, it'll be too soon.) The guys sure talked a game about the ladies, but Joe had warned me on that first morning as we undocked: "Nights get long out here, Kid. Sleep with one eye open." And I did.

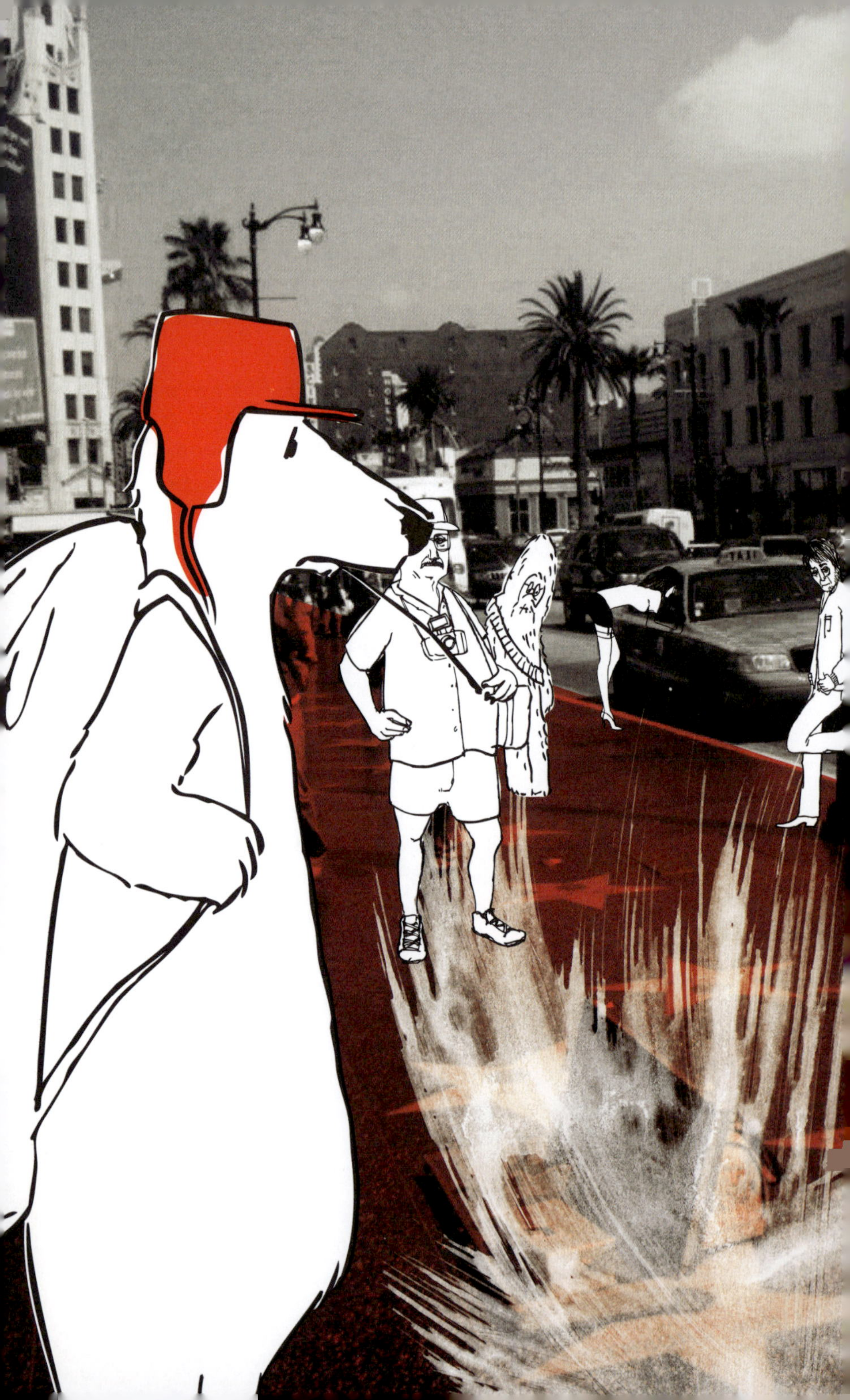

IV

Like most creatures, I've always been secretly intrigued by the palm trees and glitz of Los Angeles. After a season on the fishing rigs, working back-to-back excursions with overtime on most every shift, I figured I'd saved up enough to make my move south. Everything I owned fit in one duffel, so I threw it over a shoulder, scribbled HOLLYWOOD OR BUST on a wet piece of cardboard, and started down the state highway, turning around and walking backwards anytime a vehicle approached.

The first semi trucker who stopped made me sit in his empty, rickety livestock trailer, but he took me all the way to the Yukon. The next driver had blood-red eyes and hovered over the wide steering wheel with a suspicious expression on his face, but he let me ride inside his cozy—and strangely meticulous—sleeper cab. He complained about his wife in violent, sporadic outbursts, almost as though he was angry with me. She apparently had an addiction to the Home Shopping Network—and a severe hoarding problem to boot. He stayed on the road as much to pay off her credit card bills as to escape his cluttered home. There was no room for him anymore, no clear surface even to sleep on. I just sat on his tidy bunk and listened quietly until we made it to Vancouver.

Seattle and Portland were beautiful to watch flicker by from a window-seat on the Greyhound, but I always heard they're rainy and depressing, so I kept my sights on the City of Angels. I changed buses in San Francisco, checked out the Haight and bought a massive, over-stuffed Mission burrito for the road, but then spent the bulk of the ride through Steinbeck country hovering over the toilet in the cramped restroom at the back of the bus. *What the hell do they put in those things, anyway?*

That goddam burrito repeated on me all the way to L.A., but I was so excited when my paws hit Hollywood Boulevard that I didn't care one whit. It was both everything and nothing like I'd imagined. I figured I stuck out like a penguin in the Arctic, but there were hundreds of creatures of all shapes, sizes, languages and persuasions in Hollywood. Hell, *I* was the one who looked normal! Padding down the boulevard with stars literally under my paws, it hit me: I'd found home.

I had just enough dough for first, second, and last months' rent on a room above the Frolic Palace, on Hollywood near Vine. The freezer didn't work and the carpet smelled like clove cigarettes, but Gary Cooper's star was right outside my building's front door, and it seemed like a corner of heaven to me.

V

"Three waters on twenty-two, Beaufort!" the manager hollered. It was a constant refrain since I somehow managed to land the job at Nobu.

I filled up three glasses—one-quarter ice and three-quarters water—and carefully wiped the condensation off the glasses like they showed me, then raced over to table twenty-two without looking like I was in a hurry.

The three men at the table didn't look up at me when I approached. I placed one glass in front of

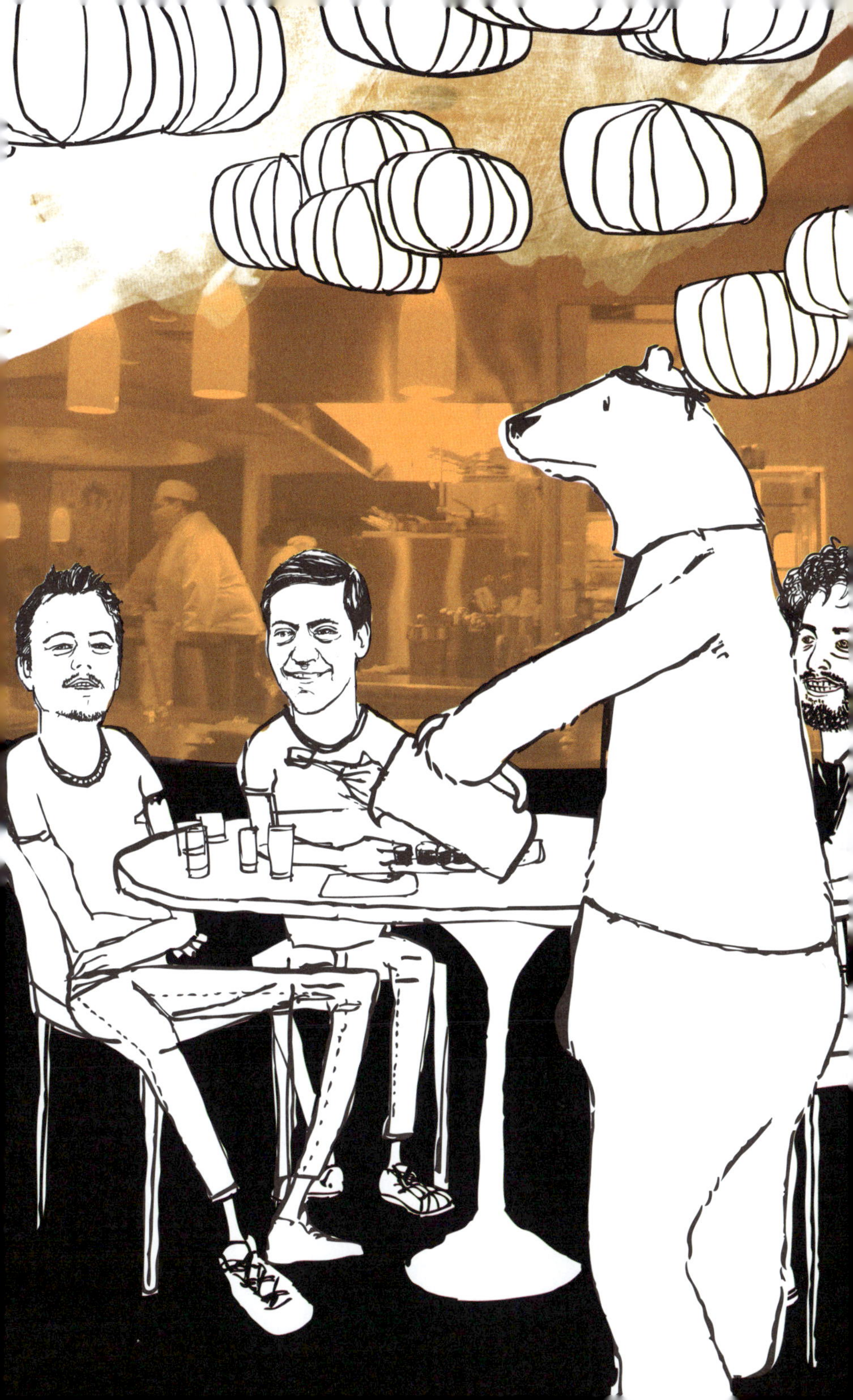

the curly-haired guy, then went around to the next one, but just before the glass reached the table, I felt something on the floor making me slip... It was one of those goddam Zen rocks that the customers rest the ends of their chopsticks on. The glass of water spilled all over the goateed guy's lap.

"What the *fuh*—?!" he yelled, bolting up and brushing the water off his expensive-looking jeans.

"I'm so sorry, so sorry," I said, but he just stood there staring at me like maybe we'd met somewhere before. His eyes were totally disarming, the hue of translucent, early-winter ice. I repeated, "I'm *really* sorry," and headed toward the staging area to fetch a towel, again trying to appear calm and centered while crossing the dining room.

"Do you know who that is?" one of the waiters asked. It was the first time he'd ever spoken to me outside of barking demands in my direction.

"Who?"

"The guy you spilled on."

"I don't know. No."

"You're *so* fired. That's Leo," he spat.

I went back to offer Mr. Leo the towel, but by the time I got to the table he was already reseated and laughing riotously with his buddies about something. The other customers in the dining room looked over, trying to look like they weren't looking.

"It's okay, man. Chill out," Mr. Leo said.

"Can you sit down for a sec?" the third, sleepy-eyed guy asked, pulling out a chair. "Let me pour you some sake."

I glanced back toward the reception area where the manager was scowling at me. "I can't, I really need to—"

"Dude, you'd be *perfect* for this film I'm doing," Mr. Leo interrupted. "Are you green?"

"I don't know," I said. "I mean, sometimes my fur turns a little green when the algae content goes up in summer."

All three of them laughed some more.

"This is Tobey, that's Adrian. And I'm Leo."

"My name's Beaufort." We shook hands and paws.

"Here's my direct line." Leo jotted a number on a chopsticks wrapper. "I'm serious. You and me, we could really make a difference."

I stared into his crystal eyes. They kind of killed me. "I gotta get back to work."

IV

I didn't have a telephone connected at my place yet, so I didn't try to call Leo. Everybody at Nobu said he was probably a phony anyhow, and that I shouldn't feel special that he gave me his personal number. But a few days after the ice-water incident, Leo's assistant phoned me at the restaurant while I was setting up for lunch.

When I came out to the front desk, the day manager hissed, "No personal calls!" as he tossed me the handset, and then as soon as I pressed the receiver to my ear, that mean waiter whisked by and whispered,

"Fired," while making a hand gesture that looked like he was slicing his own neck with a finger.

"Uh, he-hello?" I stuttered like a madman into the phone.

"Can you come in for a screen-test at four-thirty this afternoon?"

My pelt was going to have to be dyed whiter, and I'd have to learn a ton of lines in less than a week, but that afternoon the producers offered me the role of Leo's sidekick in his new movie *Separation of Oil and State*, a psychological thriller-*slash*-legal drama-*slash*-buddy flick about global warming. I was worried about giving up my job, but over a long and leisurely poolside lunch at Chateau Marmont the next day, Leo convinced me that I wouldn't need to slave away as a busbear anymore, and promised that if for some reason I ever wanted my job back, he'd help me get it.

"I can't go to Alaska," I said, taking a gulp of some bubbly water from a green bottle. It tickled my nose.

"You don't *have* to," Leo explained. "Warner Brothers is building the Arctic on the back lot."

"So I don't have to go north?"

He shook his head vehemently and mused, "For a polar bear, you sure don't *chill* very much." Then he gestured to the waiter to bring us two more sides of calamari tempura.

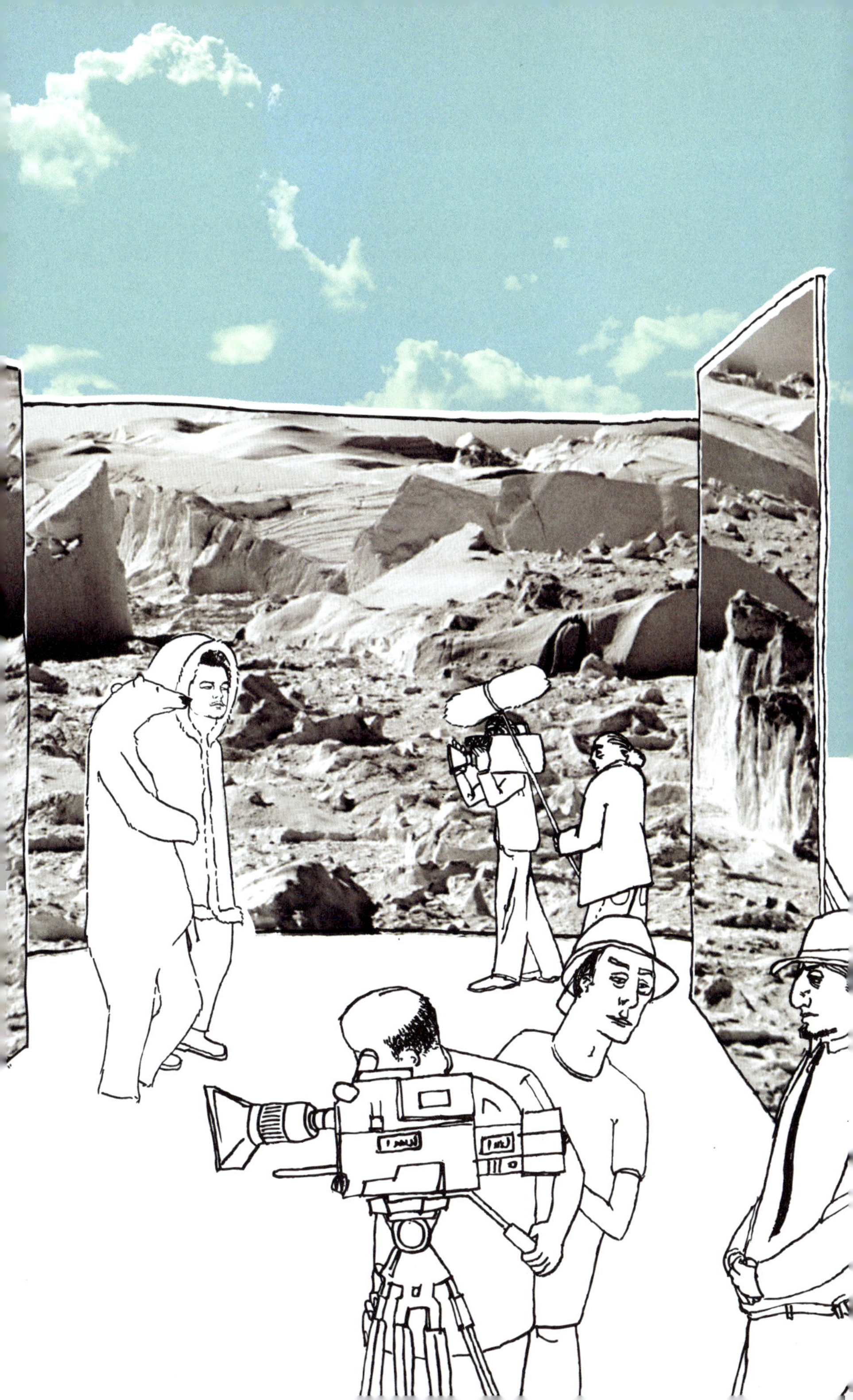

The studio put me through a me a crash-course in acting, but I was still jittery the first time we ran lines as a cast. Leo was protective like a big brother and generously helped me through some hairy spots. But after a few rounds of dialogue, all of the cast said I was a "natural" and didn't need anybody's help. Still, every night I'd go home early to my room and dutifully meditate on my character's motivation, drawing heavily on my experiences in order to imbue him with the emotional authenticity and psychological realism that weren't necessarily on the pages of the script.

The first day we started shooting *Separation of Oil and State*, it was clear that Leo and I had chemistry. People started talking Oscars, but that didn't faze us; we simply believed in what we were doing, and that made all the difference. Shooting rolled on, and I quickly ascertained that there is a lot of hurrying-up-and-waiting on a film set. In between takes we'd go back to one of our trailers and talk about life—our families, the notion of happiness, the past. It turned out we had similar relationships to our distant fathers, and strong mothers who were there for us in leaner times. Well, until recently that is, at least where my mother's concerned.

"You make your own family, B," Leo told me, and it was the first time I really appreciated the difference between the family you're born into, and the one you create. Just before we headed out to shoot another grueling scene on the ice, I asked Leo if he might like to be a part of my new family, and he replied, "You know we're bros," and we sealed it with a fist-paw bump.

VII

They say each generation seeks to surpass the one that precedes it, but I always had some degree of ambivalence around this notion. My parents had drilled it into me: live small, take no more than what you need, and give back more than you take. Nevertheless, even I had to admit that my steadily ballooning bank account wasn't quite congruent with my crumby, ice-cubeless, and cockroach-filled existence in that musty room above the Frolic Palace.

So about half-way through filming *Separation of Oil and State*, I jumped on the opportunity to lease a house in the Hollywood Hills when the Assistant Director told me about a property opening up that would be perfect for me. Everybody said the market was "insane" but that it was also the ideal time for people like us to buy. *People like us*. I wondered what my mother and her scant twenty-dollar bill would think about that. *If she could only see me now*, I chuckled to myself, as I pressed my paw-print onto the rent-with-an-option-to-buy contract on a house in the hills.

I decided to host the wrap party at my new place. We hired Nobu to cater, and damn if I wasn't just a little delighted to see that one of the staffers sent over by the restaurant was the waiter who always said nasty things to me and shorted my tips at the end of every shift. I told him he was welcome to borrow

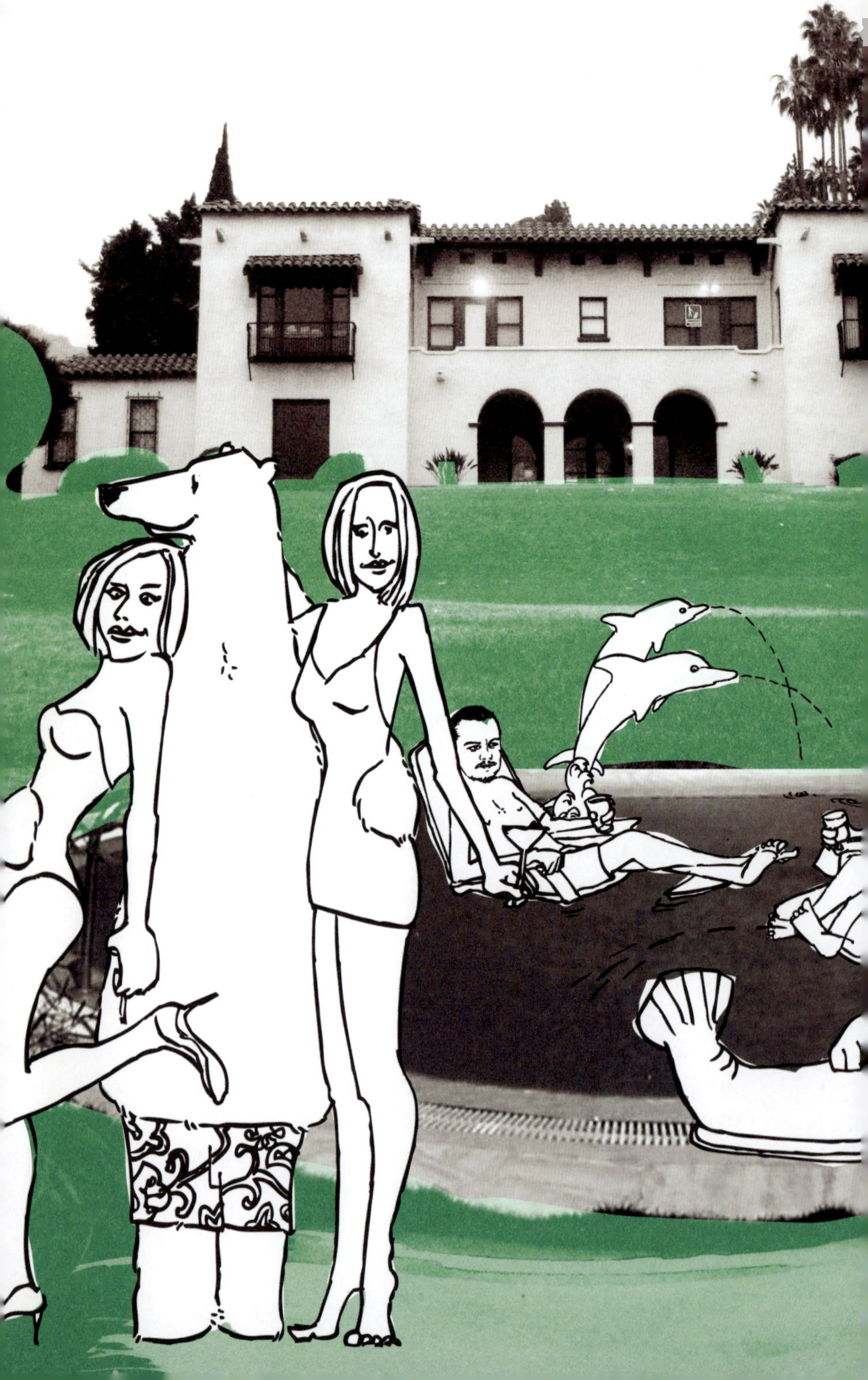

some trunks and a towel and take a swim as soon as the guests were finished eating. But he could scarcely look me in the eye.

The party eventually opened up to friends of the cast and crew, and it lasted all through the night and into the next morning. But I didn't remember much after about 3 AM. Gisele dropped by with somebody she wanted me to meet, a model named Svava, new to town from Reykjavik. After splashing around in the grotto over several rounds of strong Tom Collinses, Svava asked whether I "liked skiing, or was it just a facade?" and led me back to my bedroom, where we started getting funny on the fur rug beside the electric fireplace. Svava was nothing like the women in *Juggs*, and I never imagined anything could be as soft as her skin; it was night and day from anything the guys on the boats described.

At some point I think I mumbled to Svava that I'd just fallen half-in-love with her, and then we passed out on top of a mountainous down comforter on the floor. When I woke up the next afternoon, Svava was gone—the only remnant of her a torn pair of black stockings draped suggestively over the flatscreen TV.

VIII

It was like entering the freaking Death Star or something, getting sucked in by a tractor beam. But with Leo playing Obi-Wan to my Luke Skywalker, I marched into the Creative Artists Agency building one afternoon a cub with a modest dream and came out a raging bruin, literally and figuratively flanked by a team of agents who promised to nurture me and my dream better than anybody ever had in my life.

Music to my little orphan ears.

Did you know they have a secret entrance at the DMV? I didn't, but boy, when Leo is your designated driver, you go in through a private side door, and twenty-five minutes later (after satisfactory attempts at parallel parking, successfully indicating and completing your turns, and changing lanes relatively uneventfully), you drive off the lot blissfully, terrifyingly solo in your new Toyota Prius hybrid—tricked out with DVD player, built-in Bluetooth, satellite radio, leather seats, fresh custom rims, and my favorite touch: heated seats for when it gets chilly. In fucking L.A.!

The car was a gift from the producers of *Separation of Oil and State*, which was in post-production and still getting what many were calling, in hushed tones, "unprecedented buzz." Apparently, the phones had started ringing for me at CAA, too.

"Who is Beaufort?" One of my agents' assistant's assistant called on my Blackberry to ask while I was driving on the 405 freeway between meetings one afternoon.

"Th-this is Beaufort?" I stuttered in the direction of my Bluetooth mic, which I was never confident actually picked up sound. All I could hear through the speakers was staticy cackling.

"No," she said. "Who *is* Beaufort? Everybody wants to know."

The night after our *Rolling Stone* cover shoot, Leo and I took the girls out to the Roosevelt for a private party. Svava was just back from Milan, and she was in one of her moods, disappearing frequently with some of the birds from *The Hills* into one of the V.I.P. guest rooms and staying gone for long spells at a time. But I was getting my drink on, and wasn't going to allow anything to stop me from letting loose that night.

I decided to take a swim and for a nice long while floated happily in the middle of the glowing pool, listening to the frenetic cacophony of all the partiers. Watching the guys' wallet chains twinkling, and the girls' tight t-shirts straining to contain everything therein. Leo flashed me an ironic peace sign behind some guy's back and raised a glass—it felt like the beginning of something.

Eventually Svava reappeared, teetering alongside her twiggy model friends, and as always when I saw her anew, I felt that flush in my chest when our eyes first met. "Over here, baby," I hollered across the silky surface of the pool, trying to reel her in with one of my sexy looks she'd always said she likes so much.

She never came over though. So I just kept bobbing and watching. We left early. And Svava didn't say anything to me for the rest of the evening, except one thing, right after the valet slammed the car door behind her: "Nobody actually swims at these things, Beaufort."

IX

When things were good with Svava, they were really good. But when things were bad, it was lousy. All along though, our intimate life was a constant wonder. I'll try to be a gentleman and maintain some modicum of discretion here, but: the girl was *hot*—and knew what she was doing. We made love for hours at a stretch, passed out in each other's arms and then woke up and did it all over again. I never imagined two bodies could melt together like that, and she said she'd never been with a creature like me, that she couldn't imagine ever wanting anything else. I never thought I'd hear anything like that from another being in my entire life. It was intoxicating, verging on addiction—and I can't front: I was cuntstruck like the guys on the fishing boat predicted I'd one day be. Svava was nothing less than my whole world.

But eventually Svava's focus strayed from me and honed in on herself, her body specifically, about which she said hateful things on a constant basis. I noticed new cuts and scars on her stomach from time to time, even though she tried covering them up with thick make-up and insisted she'd just been accidentally scratched on a couple rugged outdoor bathing-suit shoots. When we had sex, she asked me to make it hurt, and afterwards she'd get out of bed and stand in front of the full-length mirror, a blank expression like a white shade across her face. She'd tent her belly skin between fingertips and whisper robotically, "I think my butt's getting big." She started eating even less than she had been when we first met, and after work trips to Europe she came back toting more and more of the white powder we occasionally dabbled in on special occasions.

Every day, it seemed, was becoming increasingly "special" to Svava.

I tried to console her with stories about how where I came from, packing a little extra meat was an asset, a matter of survival, but it seemed only to inspire more rage toward me and self-loathing in her. Soon she stopped wanting me to touch her altogether, brushing me off with a half-serious, "Stop pawing me." Which only served to make me feel inadequate, like what Svava really wanted was a "real" man again—the kind she'd always been with prior to me. When I'd intimate as much, she'd deliver an obligatory, "You're the perfect boy for me"—and on my better days I almost believed her.

Still, after we ran into one of her exes—some surprisingly short reality TV host with spermicidally-frosted hair highlights and calf implants—at a club one night, I tortured myself for weeks afterwards. How his pillowy lips brushed her cheek when they hugged, how she giggled like an imbecilic school girl at that douche's stupid global warming jokes and goofy dance moves, his "rounds of Smirnoff Ice for everybody!" I stood off in the wings watching it all, seeing so much red it eventually turned searing white behind my eyes. That hairless, muscular build, how his butt looked in saggy, ridiculously expensive designer jeans—things my body could never do or be. *Is that what she wants?* was the constant refrain in my brain.

Kabbalah helped all that. Svava came home the morning after one of our epic fights with a piece of red string and tied it around my left wrist in seven knots. She said she knew I'd experienced the ultimate rejection when my mother let me drift away from her on that ice floe, that it affected how I treated Svava, the first woman in my life after my mother. The red string technology was supposed to remind me that I could always look down and feel the warmth from the matriarch of the world, Rachel, whose greatest desire is to defend all of her children from evil.

At the Kabbalah center on Robertson I met so many other folks who were also struggling to understand past wounds and deconstruct histories of abandonment. Svava and I started attending regular classes and study groups together, and as a result started relating on a level we'd never before imagined possible. Demi and Ashton became mentors and "couples" friends. I'll never forget one night out at the Ivy, when Demi leaned in close, put a hand on my forepaw, and told me that I might not know it then, but that soon I would need a spiritual inoculation against negativity and jealousy on the

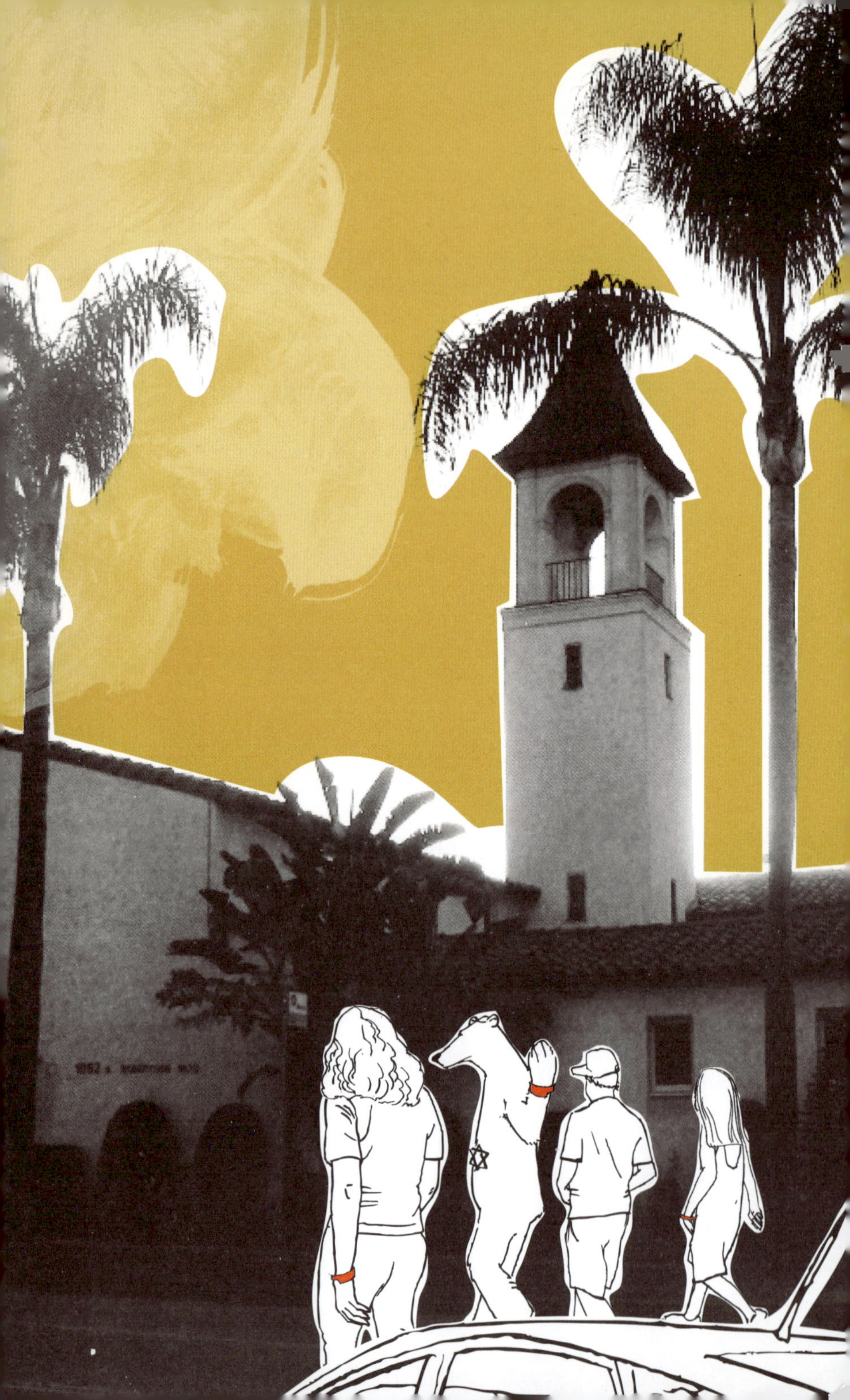

part of others, with which the bracelet would definitely help. That "Beaufort" would soon become a household name, and not to be surprised if the Evil Eye was soon to follow.

X

On the afternoon of our premiere, we all met up at Leo's place, and the two of us poured a couple scotches while the girls finished getting ready upstairs. The producers wanted us to show up to the event in our Priuses, so I offered to drive because I'd just had mine detailed.

"Bro," Leo laughed, "this is Sam, and this is Travis. They're gonna drive us over there in both our cars."

"Oh, duh," I said, feeling stupid. Travis leered at me from beneath his tight, curly mohawk. And I think that's when it hit me. How different everything was going to be from here on out. What Demi said. How life just changes in the flash of a klieg light like that. It seemed like I should be excited, but the revelation just filled me with about eighty percent anxiety and twenty percent sadness. I guess I was becoming quite a nervous guy back then.

"Fix your tie," Leo said, jutting his chin toward my neck, and then I heard Svava's heels on the stairs, and when I turned to look, she was simply radiant and I couldn't take my eyes off of her, the uneasy heaviness in my chest replaced with pulses of something warm and syrupy swirling around inside. Then Svava did something she hadn't in some time: reached over

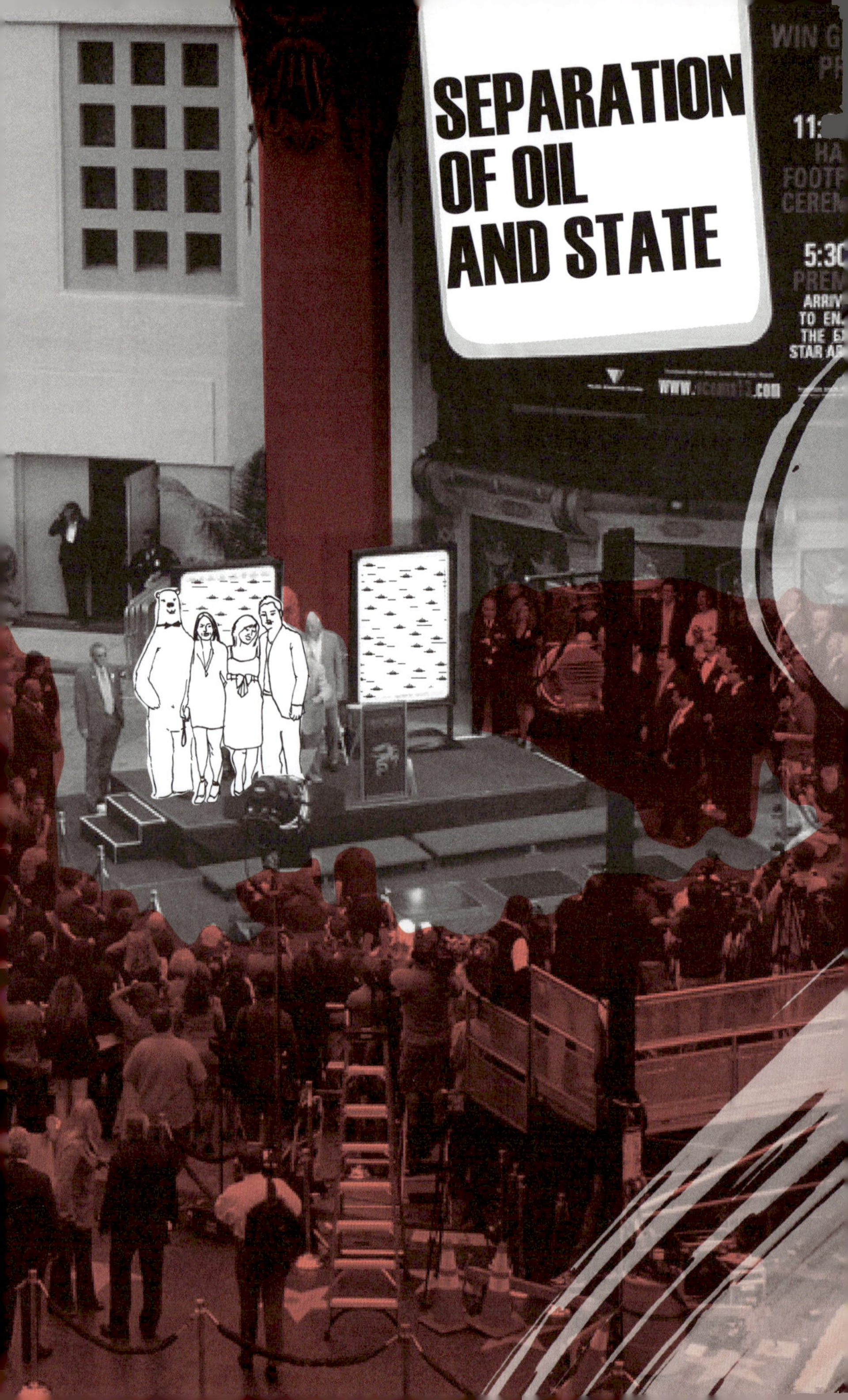
SEPARATION
OF OIL
AND STATE

and squeezed my paw as we headed out the door to the cars. She didn't actually say it, but it seemed like she was a little proud to be on my arm that night.

Leo snuck out before the screening began, but I saw the film for the first time all the way through. It was almost like watching a really good actor playing me, but the handshakes and pats on the back at the after-party confirmed it was indeed just little me from the Beaufort Sea up there on that screen. "Surreal" doesn't begin to describe it. And the reviews were, well, I was quite honored by the bulk of them...

AUTHENTICITY ON A SCALE HERETOFORE NEVER CAPTURED ON CELLULOID.

DICAPRIO AND THE NEWBIE BEAUFORT SIZZLE IN THIS COOL NEW FLICK.

BEAUFORT PUTS A FORMIDABLE YET ARTFULLY SUBTLE FACE ON CLIMATE CHANGE.

WHERE'D THEY FIND THIS GUY? BECAUSE IT CERTAINLY WASN'T CENTRAL CASTING.

When I pulled up to my favorite newsstand in West Hollywood on the morning after the premiere, the hoary (and usually grouchy) owner came striding over to my car before I even had a chance to throw it in park. He shoved three or four magazines through the window—in addition to *Rolling Stone*—on which a shirtless Leo and I shared the cover. He refused to take my money. I sat in the car with the windows up, inhaling the dry heat and flipping through all the glossy, perfume-infused pages: my muzzle looked a little big on *Men's Journal*, the pin-striped waistcoat and pink pocket-square a little ridiculous in *GQ*, and I thought my fur seemed a little washed out inside *Details*, and—*WHAT THE FUCK?*

"But I never said my dad split when I was born, or that I grew up in the projects," I whined to Leo over the phone. "I just said that times were *lean* and I didn't see my father much."

"Did you say 'starving'?" he asked. "Did you actually use the word?"

"I don't know, maybe. Maybe I said I had *friends* who were starving—"

"Whatever, don't sweat it," he interrupted. "Par for the course. Just watch what you say from now on."

So I did.

XI

The next week, CAA called with offers for three films over the next six months. And those were just the ones they thought worthy of my consideration. When the news came, I was still in bed watching World War II naval aircraft documentaries, and Svava was taking a steam shower—I could hear it hissing on and off for what seemed like hours. I quickly scheduled a few meetings for the next morning, and as soon as I hung up the phone went in to tell Svava the good news. My nose twitched at the overwhelming smell of eucalyptus when I nudged open the bathroom door.

I could tell something was wrong the second I spotted steam pouring out of the seams around the shower door. I couldn't see Svava's body through the glass—I couldn't see anything—but when I pulled open the door, she materialized through the haze, sprawled across the blue tile floor.

"Beau," she mumbled. "My funny little beau-beau!"

"Oh my god, call 9-1-1," I hollered, "call 9-1-1!"

"I'm fine," she said adamantly, pulling herself up onto the bench, all bony elbows and knees. "And who the fuck are you talking to?"

I gestured at her face.

"What?" She was getting angry.

I touched a paw to her nostril and withdrew it, so she could see the spot of blood on my fur. "It's nothing," she slurred, wrapping herself in a big white towel and disappearing into the walk-in closet.

When she woke up a few hours later, I convinced Svava to cancel her plans for the evening and stay in with me. I suggested I'd whip up some wheatgrass omelets and millet smoothies at the house, so that we could just hole up and unplug from it all and watch trashy DVDs all night: *Showgirls, Youngblood, Born on the Fourth of July*—a regular howl-fest. When she reluctantly agreed, cracking just a sliver of a smile, I jumped into the car and headed down the hill to Whole Foods, before she could change her mind.

I was perusing the fresh seafood and spotted some salmon that looked pretty good. *For salmon.* "So, is this wild-caught?" I had just asked the fishmonger, when I heard the most piercing screeches imaginable, coming from somewhere behind me. I didn't know if it was animal or human or vegetable or what, but then two teenaged girls approached, all shakes and quivers.

"Can we get a picture with you?" the larger of the two asked, starting to cry.

"Uh, sure," I said, taking the wrapped salmon and tossing it into my cart. I put an arm around one girl while the other aimed a cell-phone camera at us.

"Do you know Nick Jonas?" she asked, squeezing in closer.

"Nope."

"What about Zach and Cody?"

"Who?"

"Miley?"

"My turn!" the other one said, handing the camera off to the one I'd just been photographed with. Before I knew it, the new girl put her arm around me and her breasts were pushed up against my flank, and they were so large and insistent, and I don't think she could've been a day over thirteen. *What do they feed kids these days, anyway?*

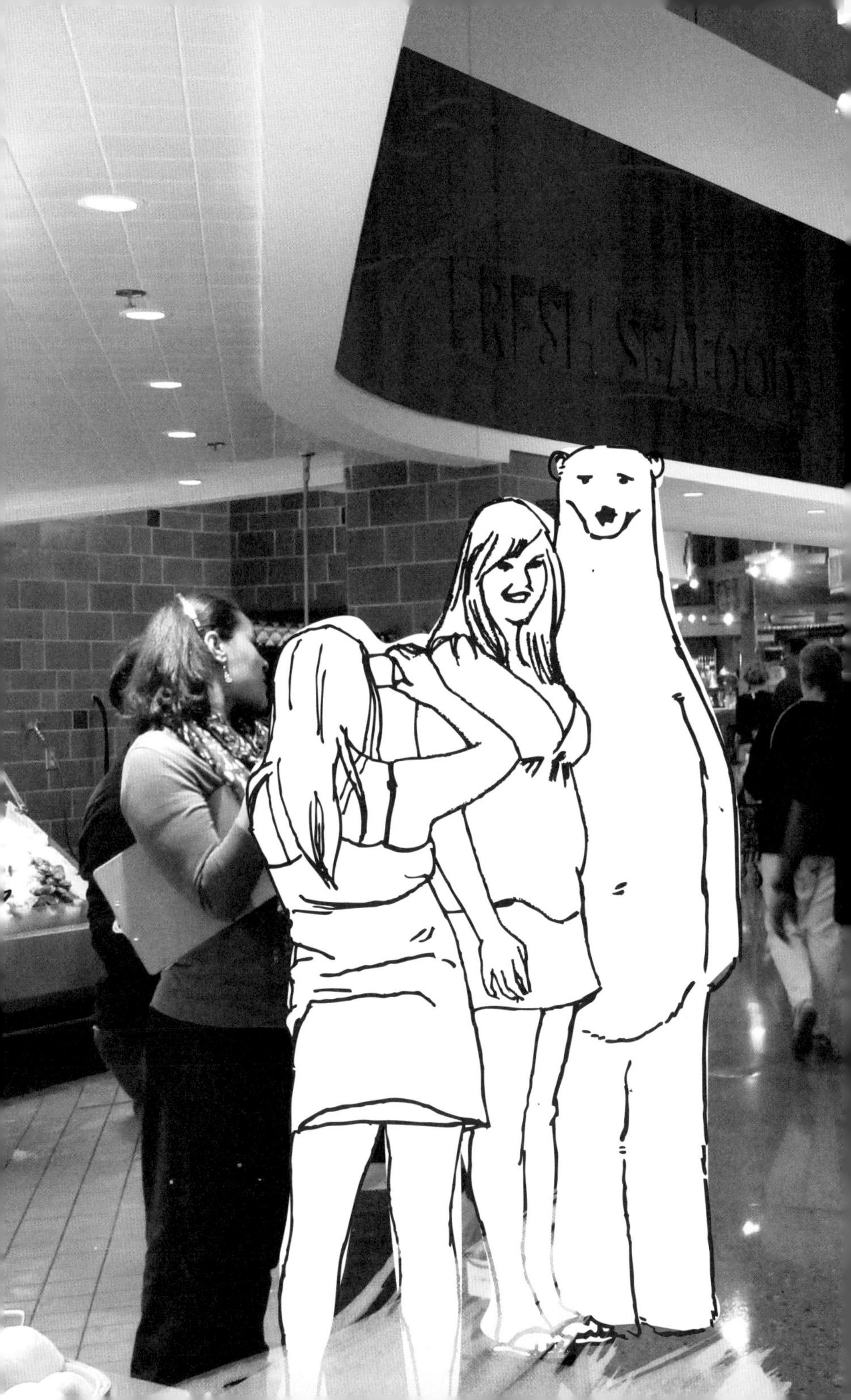
FRESH SEAFOOD

XII

BEAUFORT: CAN'T KEEP HIS PAWS OFF THE JAILBAIT

Before I even slid the salmon out of the oven, those goddam photos were burning up the internet, and my cell was ringing non-stop with calls and texts. Svava's, too. One of her friends even e-mailed a picture, and when I went to fetch her for dinner, I found Svava hunched over the laptop in my office, furiously clicking through the story on TMZ.

"Nice. Really nice, Beau."

"What?"

"You're such an idiot," she spat. "It says here other customers saw you touching this girl's privates 'inappropriately.' "

"Come on—"

You think it's a huge conspiracy, they're all lying?" she shrieked.

"Can we talk about this like reasonable people? These girls just came up—I was minding my own business in the seafood section."

"I don't care if you were in the fucking tofu aisle!"

"You actually think I was scamming on some twelve-year-old with huge boobs?"

Needless to say, I ate alone that night. And Svava called her agency to be booked on a job starting in Paris the next day. She completely iced me out, and it felt more familiar than I was willing to admit right then. I didn't know if or when I was ever going to see the girl again. And the thought paralyzed me.

After three days of not hearing from Svava and attempting to cope by abusing a few Value-Pak sized bottles of cherry Nyquil and neglecting to get out of bed for anything—not even food—my agents convinced me to take a meeting with Nicole Kidman about *The Golden Compass 2: The Return of Whimsy*. She and the producers wanted me to reprise the role of the armored warrior bear. They wanted to abandon animation for the character, and they were willing to pay handsomely for it.

At the meeting I got the full-court press, with seal-meat sushi, imported fresh by private courier jet from The Beaufort Sea, and elaborate film clips and projections and figures and promises of an even more central role in the final installment of the trilogy in a couple years. In the middle of the session I glanced over at my agent, and he was smiling so smugly and nodding his head blindly to everything that was being said, practically already calculating his fucking commission on the deal. For fielding a few phone calls, reserving the boardroom, and texting his actress/waitress/model girlfriend while nominally "taking" this meeting with me.

But I wasn't impressed by any of it. And it wasn't a done-deal like everybody assumed. Like I'm some neophyte from the tundra drooling uncontrollably whenever a few stacks are waved in front of my dis-

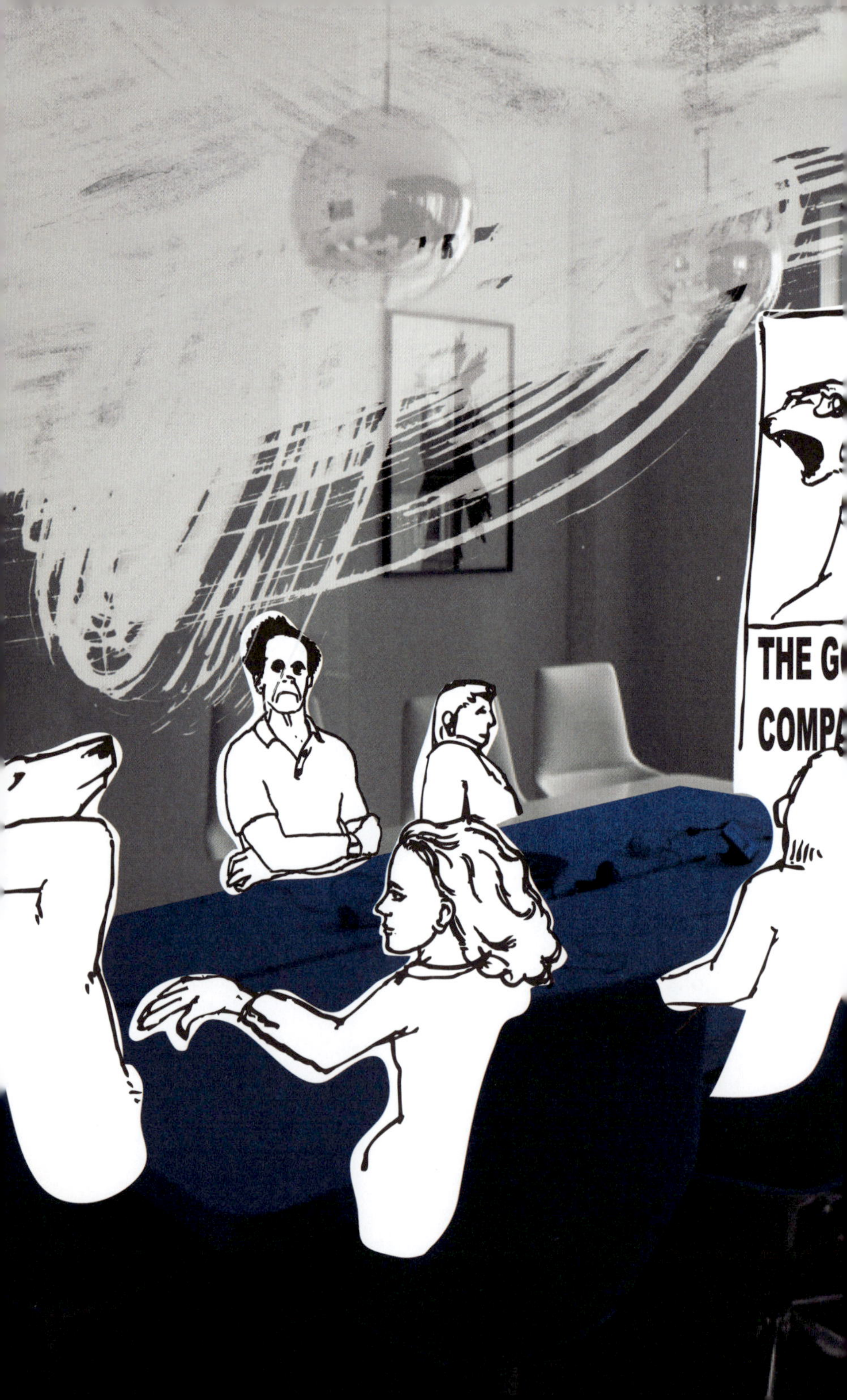
THE G
COMPA

advantaged eyes. In fact, I didn't really give a shit, and all I really wanted was to take another nip of Nyquil and climb back in bed for the rest of the afternoon and week, month, year.

As the meeting wound down, Nicole sensed my ambivalence and turned to me, earnestly declaring in that phony, reedy voice of hers: "I believe this role was *made* for you. And you were made for *it*."

"Just think about it," one of her producers added by way of punctuation.

"Oh, I will," I began, sighing. My agent shot me a look, the first time he'd registered anything all afternoon. "But I'm just not sure I want to be typecast as a polar bear for the rest of time."

Everybody shot looks at one another across the table, like, *Well, what the fuck are you then?* And it was so obviously limiting and condescending and showed such a lack of faith and imagination, and it made me want to throw up a middle finger to each and everyone of them, more than sign on any dotted line.

"What I'm really hoping to do is write and direct," I said flatly.

XIII

After I sleepwalked through another week or two in a Nyquil haze, Leo and Tobey showed up one day with a few of the other guys and tons of supplies. They threw open the windows, stuffed the kitchen cabinets with food, fired up the barbecue, and set the blender buzzing with some high-octane frozen margaritas. It was a sparkling seventy-two and sunny Los Angeles winter day, and we sat by the pool in our shades, took a bunch of dips, and shot the shit for hours about any and everything *but* work.

After a few hours and at least as many drinks, I forgot about Svava and stopped longing for her to be there too. She'd only have made me anxious about whether she was having a good time anyway. But I still missed her. Shadows started creeping across the surface of the pool, and the sun was sinking behind the hill above the house—and that's when Leo slipped into the water one last time and clumsily twisted his frame around a pink water noodle, floating there in the middle of the pool for a few beats before casually saying, "So, I brought over a stack of scripts and that software I was telling you about."

My ears pricked.

"It's shit-or-get-off-the-pot time, B."

Whenever the creative impulse struck, it'd usually be accompanied by a craving for a soy latte, so I started working on my laptop at a comfortable corner table at the Coffee Bean & Tea Leaf in West Hollywood. With Svava out of both town and contact more often than not, and the artistic bug occupying increasingly more real estate in my brain, I kicked the cherry juice habit and forced myself to keep regular office hours at the coffee house. I started off by reading tons of screenplays and taking copious notes on them; eventually I progressed to brainstorming and jotting little exchanges of dialogue and scenes, and then banging out a general three-act structure for my movie, like Syd Field suggests in his books.

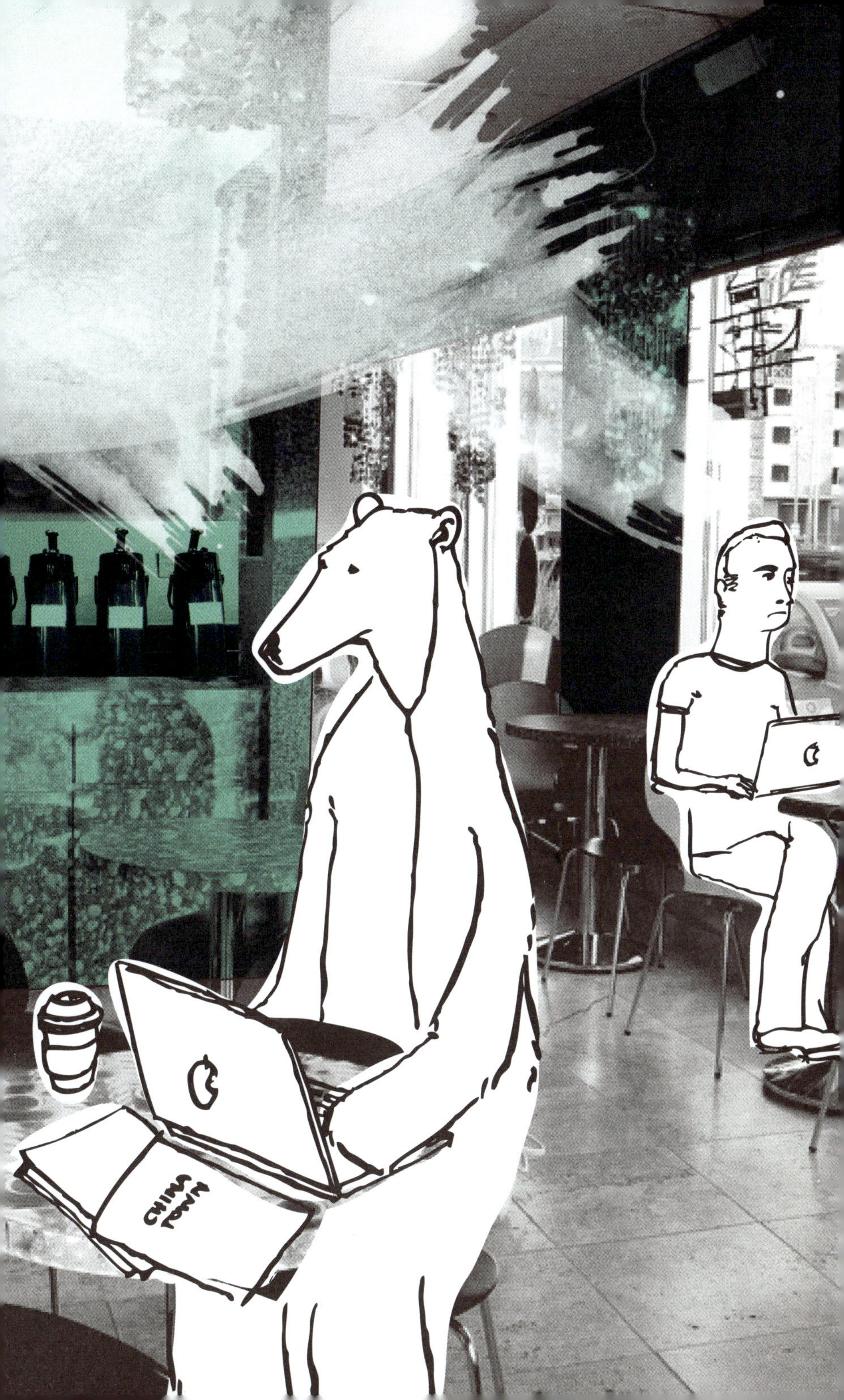
CHINA
TOWN

The idea of putting my silly snippets of ideas into 120 pages of script was entirely daunting, but at that point I could get a meeting with any writer in town, and the few I had lunch with were all very encouraging and helpful. David Benioff suggested screenwriting was "easier than bedding a woman with Daddy issues," while Diablo chirped, "I wrote *Juno* between shifts at Scores one night." Mamet said, "Go fuck yourself, you fucking faggot." So after a minor crisis of faith and another couple weeks of no-pressure doodling around on the computer, I mastered the screenwriting software and started to imagine my film in script form.

The pages flew off my paws—I'd have sucked down four lattes and three bagels with tofu-raisin cream cheese before I'd look up and realize it was nighttime. I could even start to gauge what time of day it was by some of the other creative types who frequented the Coffee Bean. At first I didn't mind when people would approach and talk to me while I worked. Some would ask for an autograph or tell me they liked my work, and others were actors or writers like me, and we'd share strategies and problem-solving techniques for whatever scene we were struggling with that day. All of it only inspired me to work harder, to show them and everybody else what I could do, who Beaufort *really* was.

After a while the flattering intrusions felt increasingly like impositions, and I stopped clinging to the enforced structure of the coffee shop and started working at home, sometimes for eight-or ten-hour stretches at a time: Creative hibernation. I was inhabiting my skin for maybe the first time in my entire life. The writing process suited me; it felt right, really like me, like what I should be doing—dealing in my own words and not anybody else's. So it was completely against my agents', colleagues', and friends' advice, but when the final call came and I was deep into a second draft of my script, I passed on *The Golden Compass 2: The Return of Whimsy*. There would always be another offer.

XIV

Back when we were shooting *Separation of Oil and State*, talking politics was, naturally, standard fare on set. It was the first time I really opened my eyes to what was happening in Iraq, and to the geopolitical impact it would have for decades, maybe centuries, to come. All of the Iraq War films that were coming out seemed to be lacking something to me, deficient in heart or an understanding of the micro threads involved in the macro quilt. But *Bear* was to be a simple story told against a complicated backdrop—a backdrop which the film was not designed even to bother trying to deconstruct or disentangle. Much less take a political stance on.

So I was floored when the head of a major company decided to greenlight my film, *and* let me make it the way I wanted to make it. The studio was hoping to capitalize on the success of *Separation of Oil and State*, and they signed Leo for a cameo appearance, so after a few meetings in which we went back and

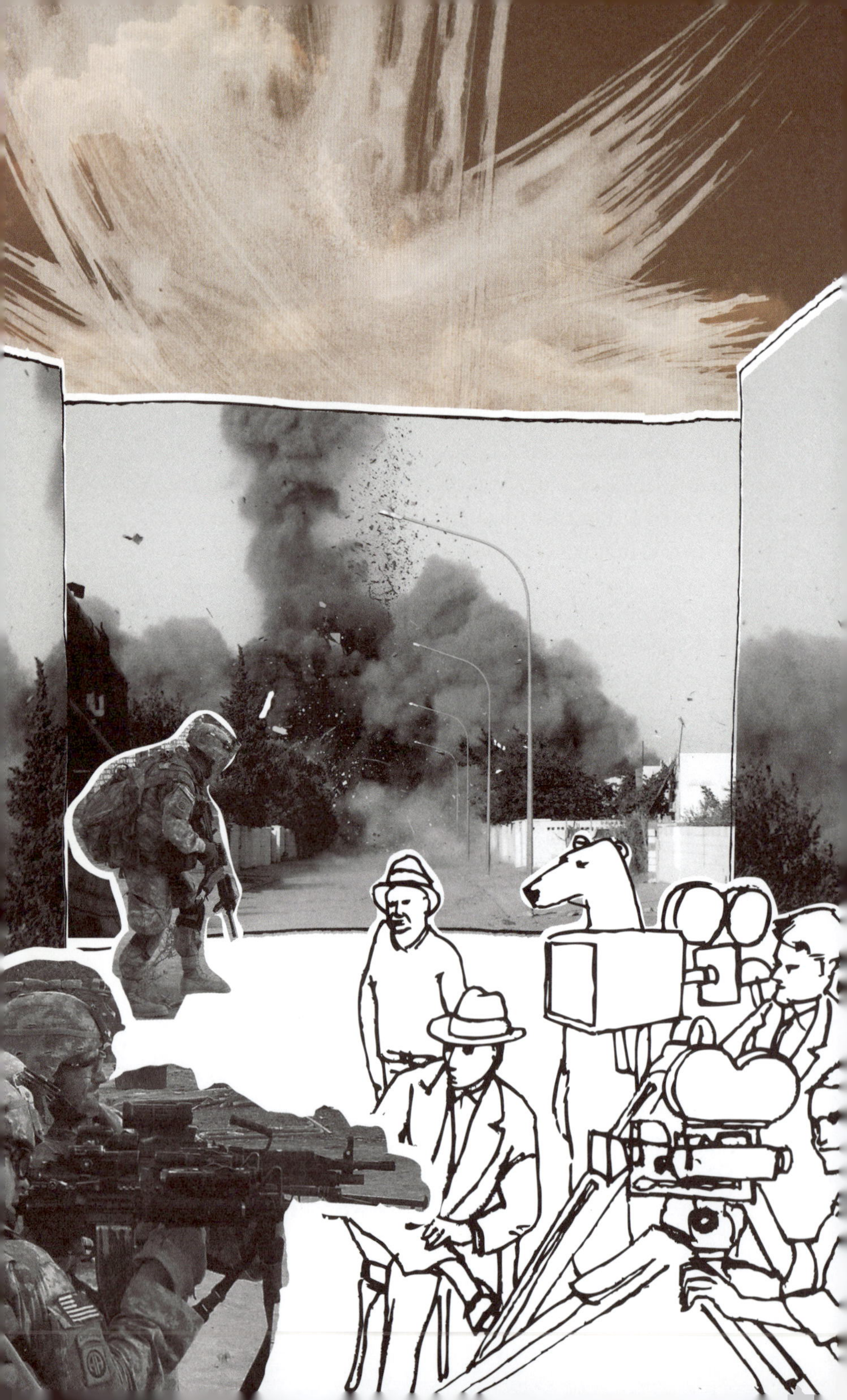

forth about the usual details, the budget people got to work and soon we were casting talent and hiring the best crew in the industry to be at my disposal.

Our first location was Morocco, to recreate most of the street and desert scenes. If I had to sum up those three weeks in Morocco, I would choose one word: HOT. It was important for me that the street fighting in *Bear* be vaguely reminiscent of the battle of Hue in 1968. It wasn't to be an overt allusion, but the Marines in Vietnam had of course been woefully unprepared for the kind of urban combat they encountered on the streets of Hue, and I wanted to faintly evoke that lack of education and fortification with respect to the 21st century Marine Corps' experience, too. I don't want to brag, but I think we nailed it.

Thousands of rounds were expelled, shit was blowing up everywhere, and guys were getting picked off in the street one after the other, their concealed blood capsules splattering in the dirt. It was just about the coolest thing in the world, the chaotic violence a controlled and intricate ballet, all in service of taking the audience on a quintessential epic journey from boy to man. I was honored to be at the helm of such a formidable project.

The rest of the film was shot in Arizona, with some interior scenes wrapped up on Los Angeles back lots. Svava actually flew to Arizona to join me for a week. She hadn't shown her face much in the previous months, but she seemed suddenly very interested in being a part of my life on set, often clinging to my arm or hanging on my shoulder when I was trying to motivate my actors or set up a shot with my cinematographer. It was certainly nice to be the recipient of her attention again, but I could tell that people were starting to talk about us behind my back.

When the producer made a surprise visit to the set to make some suggestions and discuss some budgetary concerns, I was a nervous wreck, and Svava knew it. Nevertheless, she was all over the producer, hanging on his every word and laughing madly even when nothing was funny. It made my communication with the producer next-to-impossible. It was also obvious she was high much of the time, but there was nothing I could or even wanted to do about it. I was so tired every day after shooting, and all I cared about when we'd wrap during the wee hours was going back to the hotel and collapsing in my quiet and clean bed, whether Svava was sharing it with me or not.

As it turned out, she netted more from her visit to the set of *Bear* than just some face-time with her supposed main man. The day before she left town, Svava let it slip that she'd just landed a speaking role in my producer's next film. And that she needed to get back to L.A. quick, because they were starting to shoot that next week.

XV
**ANOTHER IRAQ WAR FILM? WHAT WERE THEY THINKING?
WHERE'S THE LABEOUF? SHIA FIZZLES AS LABEAR
BEAR *NOT* A BULL AT THE BOX OFFICE
MISSION *NOT* ACCOMPLISHED: BEAUFORT A NO-FORT
WHY DOESN'T AMERICA WANT TO WATCH IRAQ WAR FILMS?**

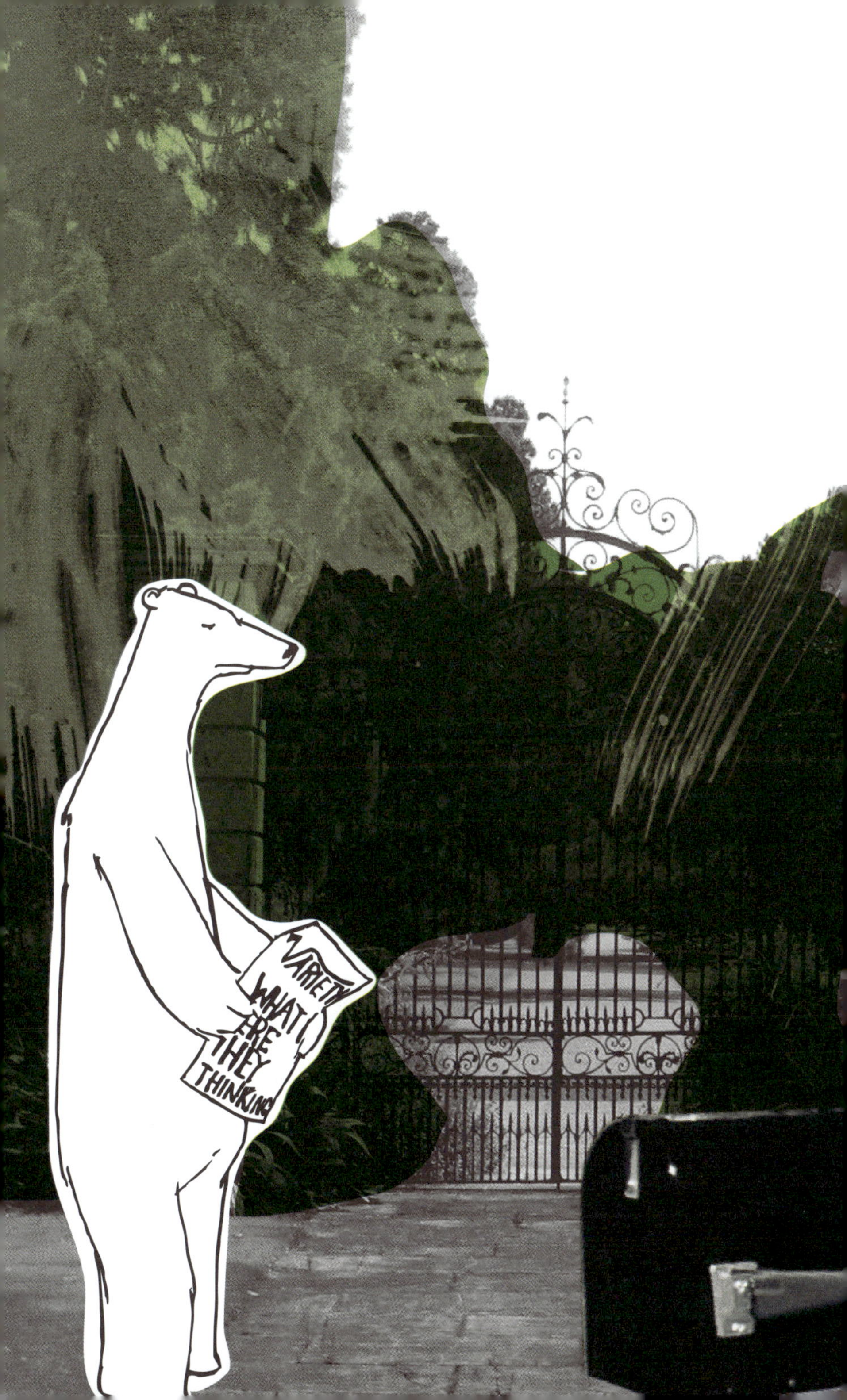
VARIETY
WHAT ARE THEY THINKING

I guess critics don't know a metaphor when they see one.

And Shia LaBeouf was in fact the *perfect* choice for the main character of Bear, the 18-year-old enlisted Marine from Alaska who gets called out by his bunkmates when they discover he secretly sleeps with a stuffed bear that he also totes in his pack throughout their deployment. That little bear ends up saving most of the platoon members' lives, but whatever—

We didn't even open in the top ten that first weekend, and after that, my agents stopped returning my calls. There was nothing we could do but ride it out and assess the damage later, they assured me; the studio had already jumped ship and was on to their next great white hope anyway. Leo was no help from where he was on location in Africa, and Svava hadn't returned a phone call, text, or e-mail from me since the night of the premiere, when there had still been so much optimism surrounding the film.

So I had no idea what to do with myself besides sit anonymously in the back of theaters all over L.A. and try to gauge audience reactions on a case-by-case basis. It was so depressing: most of the screens were running at 50% or less, and it was obvious the movie would be pulled from theaters as soon as our initial contracts ran out. I wept the first time I watched people walk out in the middle of a show.

After seeing the thing three times at three different theaters in the Valley one particularly pathetic night, I drove by Svava's condo and parked outside, sinking low in my seat and surveying her front door

for hours. At about two in the morning a black Mercedes with tinted windows rolled up, and sure enough she stepped out of it, offering a limp hand to my producer, who then accompanied her inside after glancing quickly over each shoulder.
Couldn't imagine wanting anything else but me, huh? Hell, I didn't blame her; I've seen Tod Browning's *Freaks*.

Everybody had told me, "Write your story." And I did. Or I *thought* I did. Small town Bear gets pushed out of the nest way too young by his mother, lives in the hulking shadow of an absent father, pushed around and misunderstood by other boys. Feels like he'll never belong anywhere, so he embarks upon an odyssey looking for he has no clue what, but ends up stumbling upon nothing less than his own manhood, and—most importantly—discovering that he doesn't have to be like everybody else in order to belong. How much more obvious could it get?

But of course the studio came in and fucked with everything. The more money they poured in, the more problems they teased out. Added a love story in the form of a pregnant high school sweetheart back home. A "happy" ending where nobody significant dies. A little brother with vaccine-induced Asperger's Syndrome. And I was on board with it all. Or that's what they made it seem like at the time. Like each and every goddam decision had been mine.

I was determined to write another movie, one that wouldn't be hijacked or tainted by concerns about market share or money. The only thing that assuaged the searing indignation and shame in my gut was Svava's powder. So I'd snort a little and then pound away at the laptop for a few feverish hours each night before collapsing, overdosed on exhaustion and self-loathing. But in the morning I'd blink open my eyes at the screen and it'd all be gibberish. Garbage. At which point I'd just fall back asleep and repeat the same process the next day.

XVI

When my new issue of *GQ* came in the mail I opened it right up, and who the fuck do you think I saw staring up at me with a big fat corny smile on his hairy mug? Bigfoot. That fag. Ended up taking the part of the warrior polar bear in *The Golden Compass 2: The Return of Whimsy*, "revolutionizing" the role and bringing an element of "hirsute realness" critics were saying had been missing from the first animated installment of the movie.

My paws were shaking so wildly, the leaves of the magazine shuddered in my grip. I pressed on, and there it was in the third paragraph:

> Producers say they had originally gone out to Beaufort for the pivotal role—an obvious fit—but that they were actually quite pleased when he declined. "There was a coldness to him," said one. "With the casting of Bigfoot we pushed the envelope and thought outside the box."
>
> "Bigfoot really opened me up," added Kidman. "As an actor, and as a person."

> Filmmakers believe they cracked open the polar bear character, moving in directions they had no idea were possible before the Sasquatch entered the picture.

Thus, I was blindsided by reality. Wrecked. There in the glossy pages of *Gentleman's Quarterly*, plain as snow for the whole world to see: the worst decision I'd made in my entire life. There had been no more offers. And they weren't coming either. There was no denying I was in director and actor jail, and nobody wanted to touch me. No clawing my way out of this one.

Late that night I found myself wandering Hollywood Boulevard near my old apartment, and squatting at the end of the bar in the Frolic Palace, downing 2-for-1 rum and Coke specials by the paw-full. I didn't recall, but I must've Hoovered the rest of Svava's powder stash before leaving the house because my nose was pulsing and burning and itching, and the other patrons were looking at me warily, even the old drunk I used to give dollar bills to when I first started making money.

The whole room was doing half-spins and then correcting itself over and over in my brain, and at some point a leathery lady with the crookedest teeth I'd ever seen sidled up to me and slurred through her jacked-up grill: "You're that thing from the movie, aren't you?"

I shook my head.

"No, I know it's you," she insisted, pressing her small hands into my furry haunches. "I thought you died or something." A few minutes and $25 later, she was on her knees in front of me in an alley around the corner, a dingy rabbit fur coat sliding off her bony shoulders. I couldn't relax—all I could think of was Svava and the stark contrast of this lady's grotesque mouth on me. It felt terrible, so I closed my eyes and cracked my head a few times back against the side of the building I was leaning up against. At least it was something to feel. And when I opened my eyes and looked back down, a glossy card tumbled by in the breeze and landed face-up by the lady's bruised knee:

If you are not happy with life, find out why.
Try a Free Personality and Stress Test.

Jonathan at the testing center led me to a desk and sat me down with a pencil and a sheaf of forms. He put a hand on my shoulder and squeezed, told me to be as honest as I could in answering the questions. So I got to work. Some were easy (*Can you see the other fellow's point when you wish to?*), while others I anxiously considered for a ridiculous amount of time before answering Yes, No, or Maybe (*Do you consider the modern prisons without bars system "doomed to failure"?*).

When I was finished, Jonathan poured me some barley juice and took me into a quiet booth to administer a final test on a machine he called an E-Meter. Then he asked if I'd like to hear my results. "I don't know, do I?" I joked, but he didn't laugh.

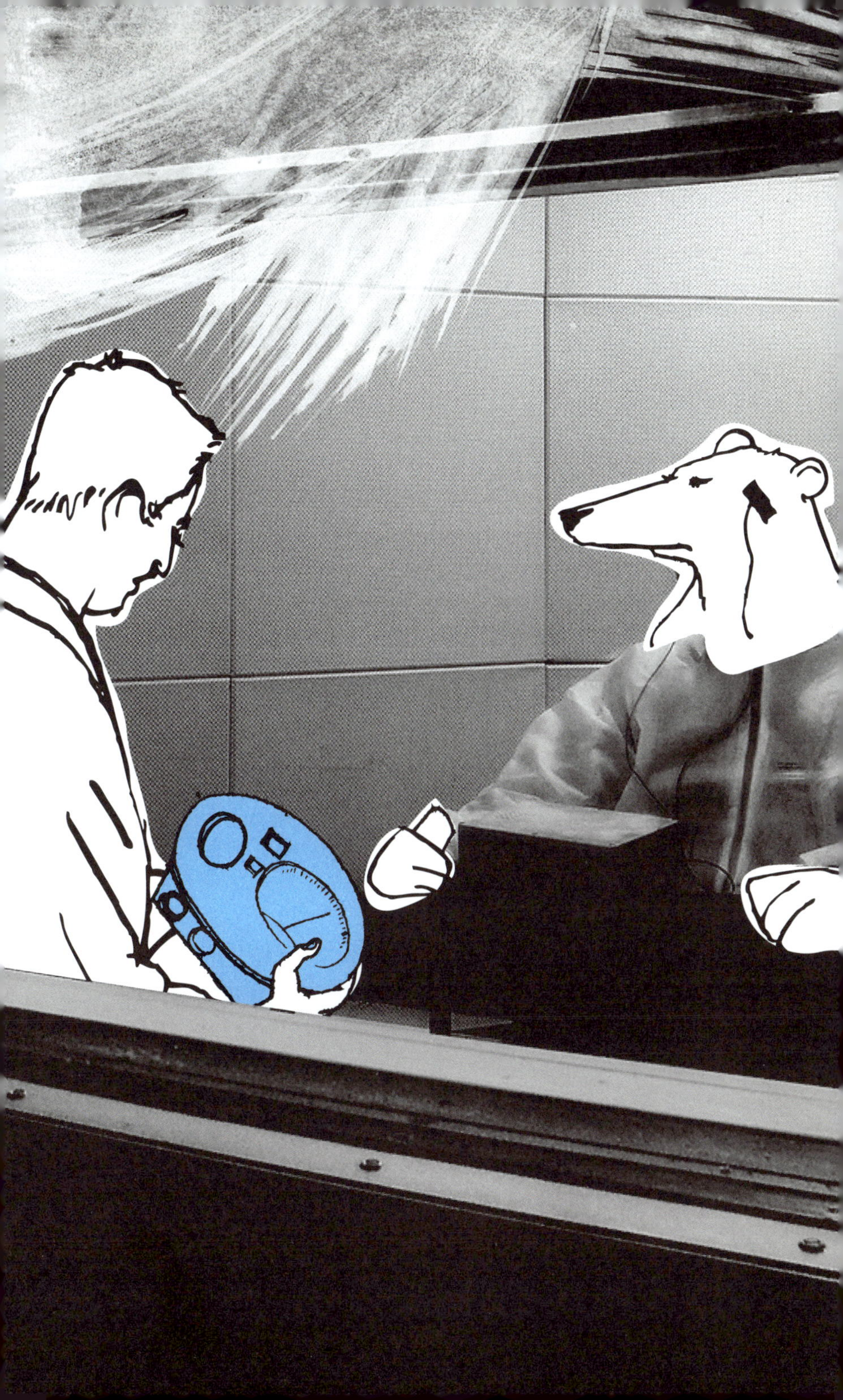

Jonathan closely scrutinized the printed out diagram for a moment and then spoke: he said it was abundantly clear from the graphs that I was deeply depressed, and also that I'd scored very low on the composure scale, which suggested to him that I tended to be a very nervous and anxious individual. Further, my responsibility score was alarmingly low, while my criticalness score was extremely high. He concluded by pointing out that while parts of my personality were very strong, others—especially those which would enhance my relationships and career—could use some serious help. He suggested a couple classes, which I enrolled in immediately using my black AmEx card to reserve my space.

I shook Jonathan's hand and promised to show up the next day for the first class. "Something's holding you back," he said, smiling enigmatically. "I don't know who or what it is, but it's seriously suppressing you, and disconnecting from whatever it is is going to do nothing less than revolutionize your life."

XVII

I figured out why *Bear* was such a monumental failure. Why *I* felt like such a monumental failure, even though by any stretch you could say I'd taken lemons and made lemonade out of my life.

At the Scientology Center I learned that the most significant *engram* of my past—when the ice broke between my mother and me—was getting in the way of my creativity and native individuality. The trauma was keeping me in a constantly *reactive* state of mind, and until I became free of those negative influences,

I would never be in complete control of my mental energy, my life, and most importantly, my emotions. I had unwittingly been feeding my reactive mind for generations and eons (even before the primary trauma with my mother), and once I realized it was the source of my fears, insecurities, pains, and nightmares, I could wrest back control of my life and eventually stop beating myself up for the failure of my movie, my relationship with Svava, and my general dissatisfaction with life.

More and more of my time and money was being spent at the Center on my auditing sessions and niacin supplements. I wasn't yet working again, but I figured I had enough savings to stay afloat for a good year or so. I did, however, trade my Prius for a 1977 Gremlin, because I was dead-set on working through the *gradients* at the Church, so I could one day get sprung from director jail and really start getting my career and life back on track—and fulfill my true unique potential. Speaking of which, CAA dropped me from my contract, but immediately afterwards the Center hooked me up with Jenna Elfman's agent, who promised to find me some pay gigs while I traveled along the *Bridge to Total Freedom*. My only hope was to become *Clear* and be introduced to the Operating Thetan levels of the Church one day.

I spent a great deal of time on the freeway in my Gremlin. It took longer to get across town to auditions and interviews of course, because I couldn't use the Diamond lane anymore without a hybrid vehicle or carpool. My new agent kept me busy with several commercial auditions—Klondike Frozen Novelties,

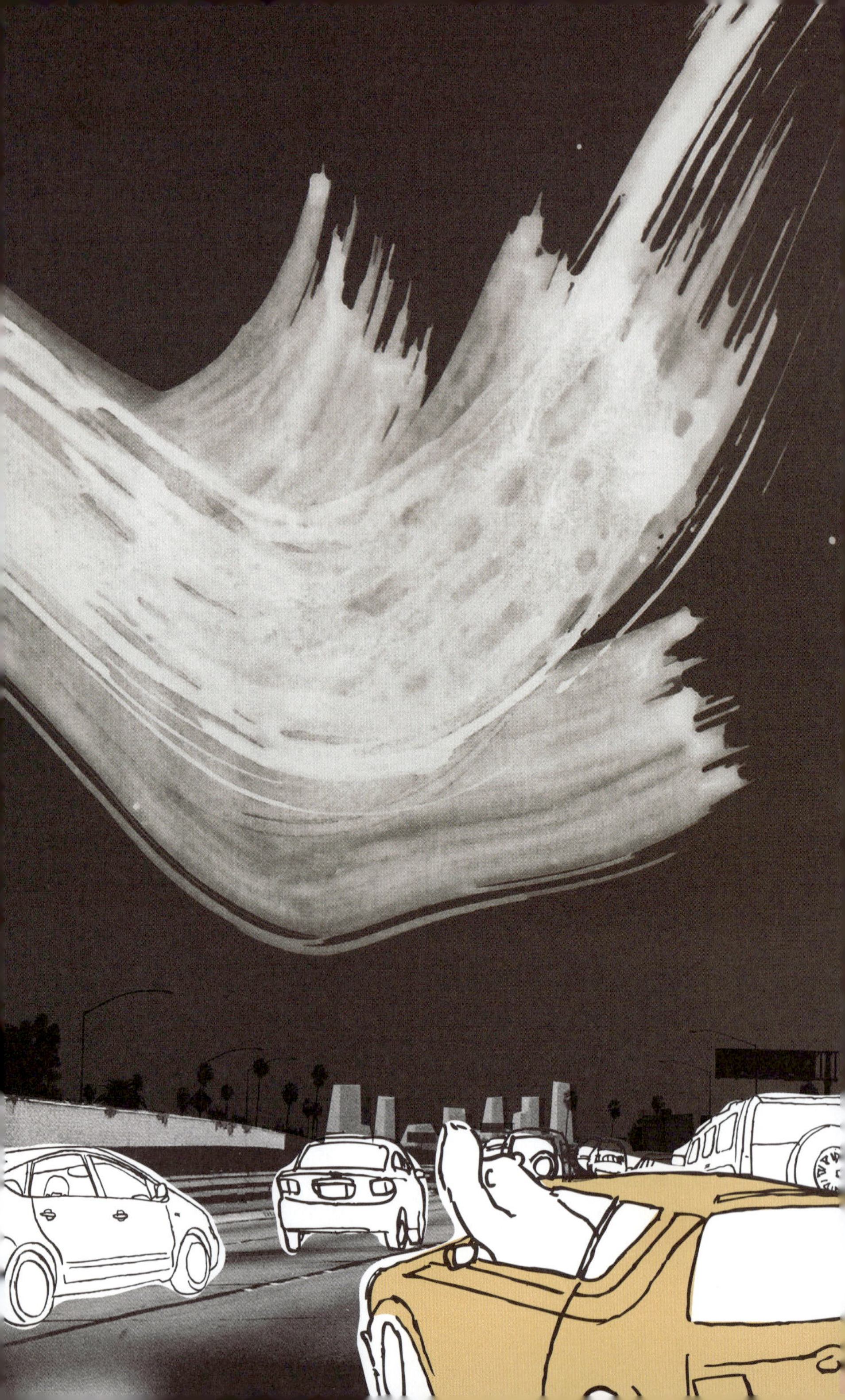

Larry's Big & Tall, Sunset Tanning Centers—but nobody seemed to want me to shill their products. Not even the reality show "I'm a Celebrity, Get Me Out of Here" would bite. "Too urban," they told my agent.

I did finally get cast in a play at a small theater in Silverlake. It was a post-colonial musical revival of the 70's TV show *The Jeffersons*; the director thought it would be an interesting twist to cast me as the Jeffersons' British next door neighbor Harry Bently. I mastered the accent and enjoyed the simple quotidian routine of rehearsals and nightly performances, but even with a few positive, well-placed reviews, the production lasted just half of its intended six-week run.

XVIII

My money ran out sooner than anticipated. The landlord was sending weekly eviction notices. I couldn't pay the pool guy or grounds man anymore. Worse, I wasn't allowed to participate in as many, or really any, auditing sessions at the Church. I was told that I could return to the center as soon as my finances were back in order, which would be a more appropriate and conducive time for continuing my journey to becoming a Clear anyway.

Things fell apart after that.

The new agent dropped me. "You're not a closer, Beaufort," he said.

This was after he'd begged a friend of a friend to give me one last chance at a corporate gig in San Diego. I was hired to be the talent and color for the

Southwest Regional Applebee's Managerial Conference, being held at the Airport Holiday Inn one spring weekend. On the first night I was asked to host their awards ceremony, and the rest of the time I was supposed to enliven the cocktail parties and dinners, chat with spouses poolside, and just generally make people feel positively about their careers with Applebee's.

I didn't last through the first night. I guess I had a little too much to drink at happy hour, so by the time I got up on stage and handed out the first award of the evening ("Most Welcoming Front End," which went to the guy at the helm of the Reno/Sparks franchise), I was a little tipsy and mostly unable to follow the script they'd given me for the evening's festivities. At some point I guess I started ad-libbing and *might've* called the vice president of the company's wife a "twadge," but I don't really remember.

Friends stopped coming around, too—well, at least the kind of friends you'd want hanging out at all hours of the day. Leo would check in from time to time, but mostly left me to my own devices, and in the vacuum some opportunistic, bad-news seals I knew peripherally from my early days in Hollywood moved into my house and took up residence by the pool. Now I knew what Dennis Wilson of the Beach Boys must've felt when the Manson family roached up on his Sunset Boulevard estate, smoked or snorted all of his drugs, and ripped off his gold records.

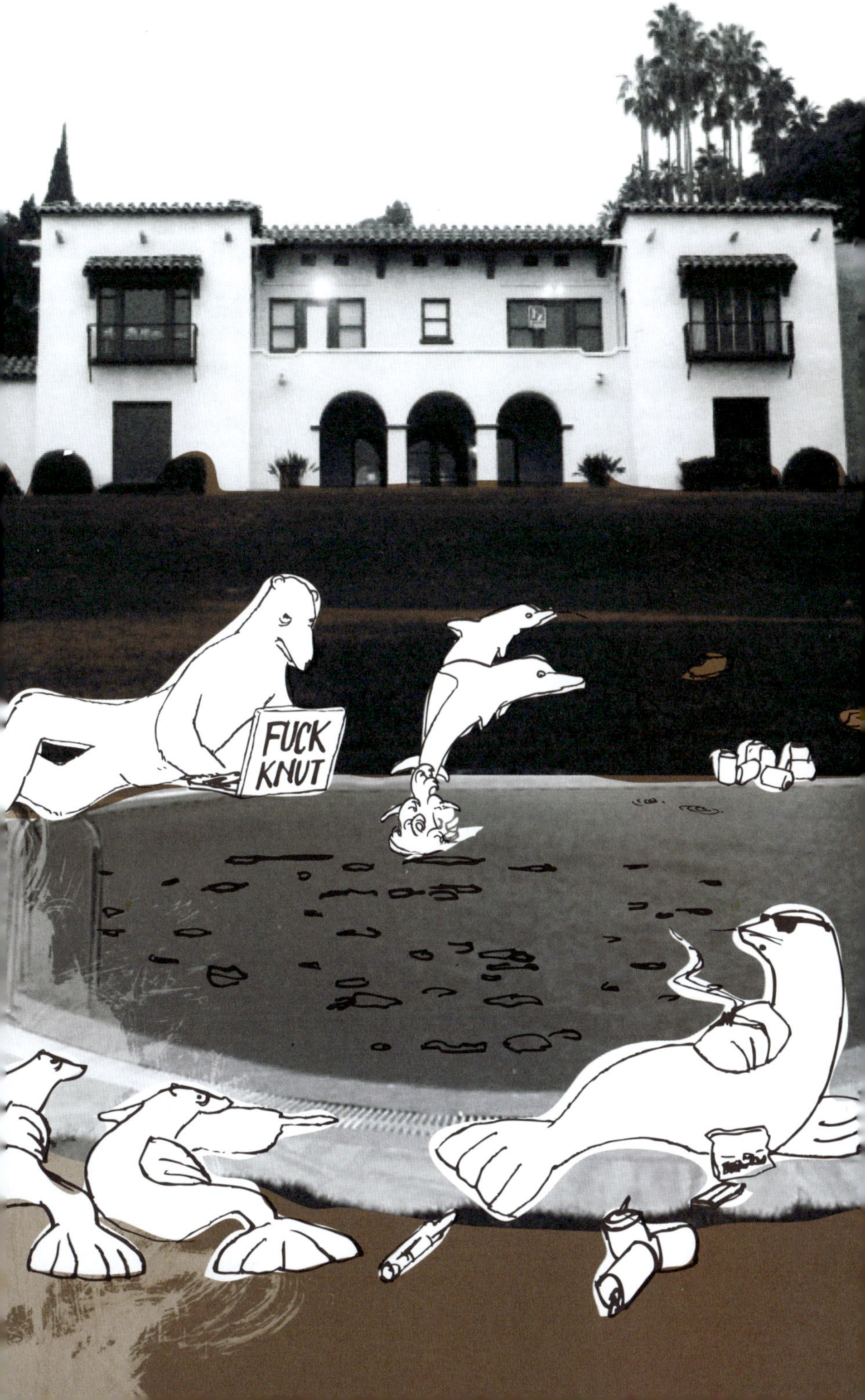
FUCK
KNUT

But what could I do? If not for the seals, I would've been completely alone in this world.

It was the seals in fact who gave me the idea to start a blog. At first it was designed to offer an inside look at the Hollywood lifestyle, from the perspective of an up and coming talent like myself. But the only interviews I could secure were with Tara Reid and Dina Lohan. Bigfoot said *No*, Ashton too, even Kathy Griffin declined—and none of my old "buddies" ever showed up or answered their phones at the agreed-upon times for our interviews.

So the blog skewed negative. I posted parts of my contract for *Bear* with my old studio, going line-by-line to delineate precisely all the ways they fucked me. I also posted the letter I received from CAA when they axed me. And some unflattering photos of certain individuals in, well, compromising positions. Svava was by then appearing in *Maxim*—#18 on the "50 Hot Chicks We'd Like to have Sit on our Faces" list. So when a topless photo of her from my blog earned a link and some subsequent buzz from PerezHilton.com, my old producer made sure to send me a cease-and-desist letter on behalf of the entire studio. Like it mattered.

But fuck him, and fuck everybody; I posted that letter, too, and for a short time I was getting thousands of hits a day. Letters from people thanking me for exposing the underbelly of Hollywood. Even some new old fans. But that all changed after an exposé I did on supposedly "green" celebrities, (Jake Gyllenhaal and Salma Hayek each took an indigenous Inuit housekeeper—they're *so* quiet—back home with them from a recent trip to Nunavut, Canada, where they had been bringing awareness to the consequences of shrinking polar ice caps; and Robert Redford, I learned, disposes of all his old vehicles in the Great Salt Lake when he's finished with them).

But I guess messing with the *Sundance Kid* is almost as much of a no-no as messing with Oprah. My hits diminished to less than a couple dozen or so a day; even Star Jones wrote a comment accusing me of "over sharing." I did have one rather persistent stalker with a plushie fetish, but he wasn't enough of an audience to inspire me to keep the blog going. And further, my electricity and internet service got shut off at the house; I couldn't even afford Val-Paks of Nyquil anymore.

XIX

On one of my last binges before completely running out of cash, I'd scribbled a hate-letter to my mother and sent it via U.S. Mail. And here it was again, down at the end of my driveway, marked RECIPIENT UNKNOWN / RETURN TO SENDER, and sitting in the mailbox atop a stack of eviction notices and recent bill collectors' efforts. I crumpled up the envelope and tossed it in the gutter, then trudged back up the driveway to plop down beside my pungent pool for the rest of the day.

"*My* mom's a twadge," one of the seals snarled.

"Mine touched me," added another. "On my hole."

"Yeah, well my mother sold me to the Bronx Zoo," said the third, stubbing out his blunt in a cup of ghetto cough syrup.

And then it hit me: I should be in New York City! Hollywood had chewed me up and spit me out like rancid blubber. It was a terrible place filled with even more terrible people, 99% of whom are phonies. New York is where it's at. Real people with real problems. Authentic, struggling artists and musicians, and serious actors working with weighty material at bona fide theaters.

Start spreadin' the news. I'm leaving today.
I want to be a part of it: New York, New York.
If I can make it there...

I collected on my final life-line with Leo and called him from a payphone down on Sunset. I'm sure he only answered because he didn't recognize the number. Leo sounded immediately exasperated, but he claimed he was happy to hear from me, and that he'd always love and care about me, but that he didn't want to enable my downward spiral any longer. That said, he offered to wire a couple grand to help me get out to New York and secure a place to stay. But it would be the last time. I couldn't have been more grateful.

So I bought a ticket on the Greyhound, packed my original duffel from Alaska, and hitched a ride downtown from one of the Inuit maids who worked at a house down the street. I nabbed a window seat, then completely numbed out as the California desert flew by my weary eyes. I thought back to my last bus trip, the ride I took south through the Pacific Northwest down to L.A.. How much optimism pulsed through me as I peered out that window into the proud downtowns of those grey cities. How certain I was about my future, even though I had no logical reason to believe in it.

And now? All that optimism, good will, random kindness, and just plain blind luck I'd been blessed with in Hollywood? Squandered, all of it just squandered, as though everybody in the world actually gets a chance like that to soar. Hollywood *and* Bust. What an asshole I was.

Through Arizona and New Mexico I thought about getting completely clean and sober once in New York. Texas, however, found me bargaining that I could perhaps have a drink or two from time to time, just since I'd be making new friends, and I wouldn't want them to think I was weird. But by the time we blew through Arkansas and landed in Memphis for an hour layover at the bus station, I was making myself promises again to get completely dry and focus on nurturing my creative self again. My *true* creative self—not one tied to any profit-centered industry run by unimaginative sheep.

From Tennessee we cut up north through Illinois and Michigan, then crossed over into Canada from Detroit. I chuckled when I saw the slate-blue

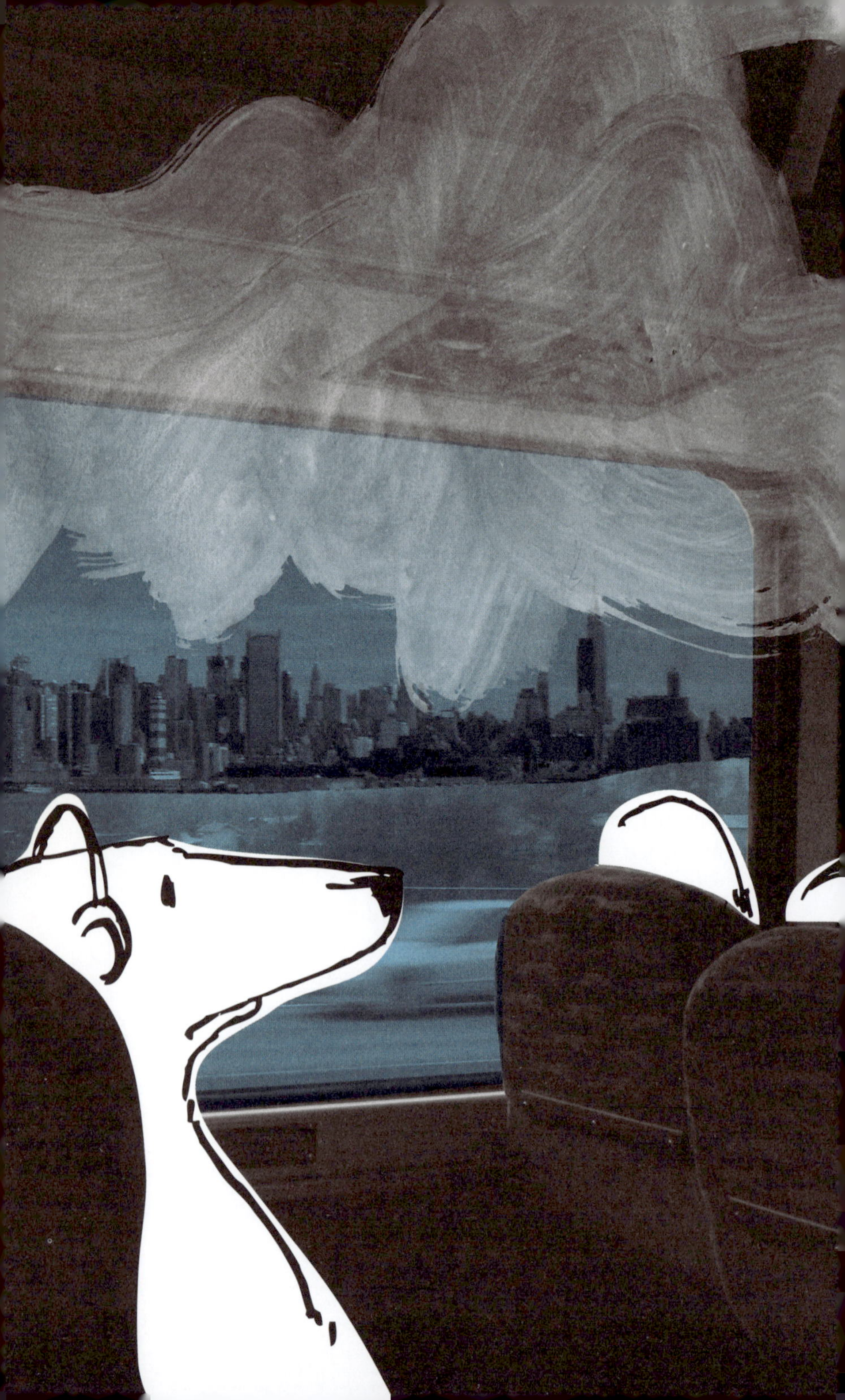

cylinders of the GM building looming over the downtrodden downtown, and realized I was listening to the soundtrack from *8-Mile* on my iPod.

> *You only get one shot, do not miss your chance to blow.*
> *This opportunity comes once in a lifetime, Yo.*

I feared that I'd indeed pussied out and let my one shot slip. So I shut my eyes in hopes of tamping down the tears, and ended up sleeping all the way through Ontario and into upstate New York; after three and a half days in the same tiny seat, my limbs were cramped, my fur was matted, and I was cranky as hell. But boy, when I woke up with my jowl pressed against the window and looked across the water from New Jersey, I caught a shimmering glimpse of the Empire State Building pointing to the sky amidst a jagged mess of buildings in Manhattan.

Holy shit. I was completely surprised to feel something in my chest—yep, there it was, a tiny ping where there'd been only hollow for so long before. The sensation was a mere fraction of the excitement I'd felt rolling into Hollywood all those years back, but at least it was something. I couldn't wait to hit the concrete.

XX

On Craigslist I found a small, cheap room to rent from a few college kids in an Alphabet City sixth-floor walk-up tenement between Avenues C and D. The guys said they went to NYU, but it didn't seem like they attended classes very regularly. One of them had a trust fund, the other two were part-time pot dealers, and they all seemed nice enough, if a little overzealous about ordering in pizza and beer and having Wii Tennis tournaments. One of the dealers, Mike, was a film student and had actually seen and liked *Bear*. He was excited to have me live with him, and even asked me to visit his screenwriting class sometime.

Finding a job, however, proved more difficult than finding a pad. I trolled up and down the avenues below 14th Street and put in applications anywhere that seemed cool—piercing places, the sock shop on St. Marks, a few nail salons, and Toys in Babeland. Most people looked at me incredulously; some suggested I was over-qualified for sales work given my history in the film industry, while others thought me under-qualified and lacking any "real-life" experience. One suspicious old broad with crazy red hair who ran a vintage store on 7th Street even growled, "I don't know; something's off about you."

Desperate, I called Nobu in L.A. in hopes of getting a letter of reference speaking to my skills as a busbear, but it never arrived at the Kinko's where I had asked the manager to send the fax. After a couple weeks with no bites, I was decidedly deflated. And broke. Plus getting hungry. I knew there were always dog cookies inside a tin outside Mud coffee shop, so on the way home with no reference letter and no prospects, I surreptitiously grabbed a few treats and popped them in my mouth when I thought nobody was looking.

"Dude, what are you doing?" a scruffy barista in a plaid vintage shirt asked. He looked a little like Leo circa *What's Eating Gilbert Grape*.
"Uh, I'm sorry. It's for my dog."
"But *you* just ate those."
"Oh. I don't know where my dog went," I said, scanning the sidewalk. "He's brown."
"I've seen you around," he said, not buying it. "I know who you are. You hurting, man?"
I didn't say anything.
"We need a dishwasher... You want me to hook you up?"

I started feeling settled at Mud and was bringing in some regular cash. One day I noticed a flyer in the shop for an upcoming mixer sponsored by Bearhunt.com. It ignited that old, familiar itch for companionship, the need for a new posse. I borrowed my roommate Mike's computer and RSVPed for the mixer, and a couple days later I heard back from somebody called PolarHole212. He asked to be my "buddy" on Bearhunt, and told me more about the party, which was going to be at a place called The Cock on 2nd Avenue. I was psyched about the prospect of meeting another actual bear in the city, and I found myself wondering what part of the Arctic this guy was from.

As it turned out, PolarHole212 was not a bear at all, but rather a heavily bearded guy named Rick from the Upper East Side, who liked to wear leather, studs and piercings, and worked for the Manhattan Transit Authority. He thought the Beaufort Sea was some-

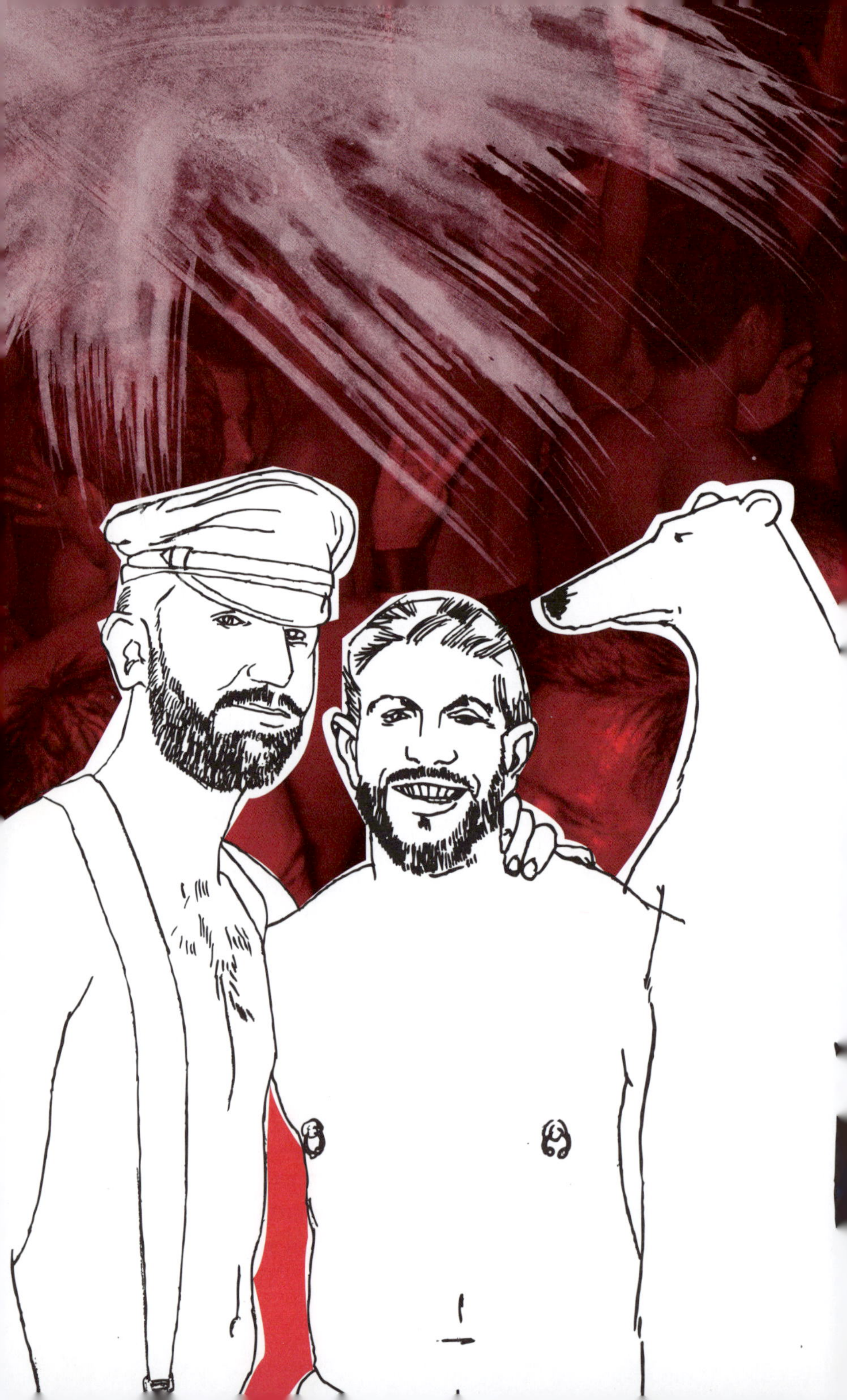

where off southern France, but no matter: Rick was a blast, and he introduced me to a bunch of his friends, and they loved to dance (I love to dance), and play rough (I love to play rough), and the drinks were always cheap and fruity and flowing (I figured a couple wouldn't hurt), and I ended up partying at different bars and clubs around the city with the guys every night I possibly could.

XXI

In time, Rick and his buddies introduced me to a little friend they liked to call "Tina." At first I just hung with her a couple nights a week at the clubs, but soon I couldn't stop thinking about her, and I'd be bumping a little in the morning before work in order to get me through each day. I wasn't sleeping, wasn't eating, and as a result losing fat reserves rapidly. I spent practically every minute in nervous anticipation of whatever festivities were planned with the boys at night, because I couldn't afford my own supply of Tina, but they always had plenty and were happy to share.

The more I used her, the more I wanted her. Because when I wasn't with my girl Tina, I found myself teetering on the edge of a pit of despair filled with shards and remnants of the mortifying disaster I'd made of life and myself. And only she could make those shameful feelings disappear, at least for a day or so at a time. Top of the world, I could dance for six hours straight and not even take a pee break or have a sip of water. With Tina I felt red-hot again, like my star was back on the rise—even if the highest it could reach was the second-floor balcony overlooking the flashing lights of the dance floor. But still, everybody downtown knew me, and I was becoming a force to be reckoned with. Indomitable.

"Beau, I think you've got a problem," Rick said to me one night when I kept bogarting all the powder and got a little too rough with some guys on the dance floor.

"Bite me—"

"No, seriously dude, we've been meaning to talk to you." He clamped a hand around my elbow, and I don't know what came over me, but at that moment I just freaked out and grabbed his wrist with my free paw and twisted it up until he was contorted underneath me, crying out in pain, "What are you doing?"

When I released him Rick dropped to the floor, rubbing his arm and grimacing like he was going to cry like a little bitch. A couple of the guys came over to check on him, all concerned looks on their furry faces. I could tell they were talking about me and scheming to come after me like some fucking vigilantes with torches and wooden stakes. But I split before they got a chance, and since I was nursing a nice high, I decided to stop by a different bar for a little while before heading back to the apartment.

I don't remember much after that—that is until waking up on a bathroom floor in an apartment I didn't recognize, with a man I didn't recognize in the other room, putting on a crisp white shirt and striped yellow tie in front of the mirror and call-

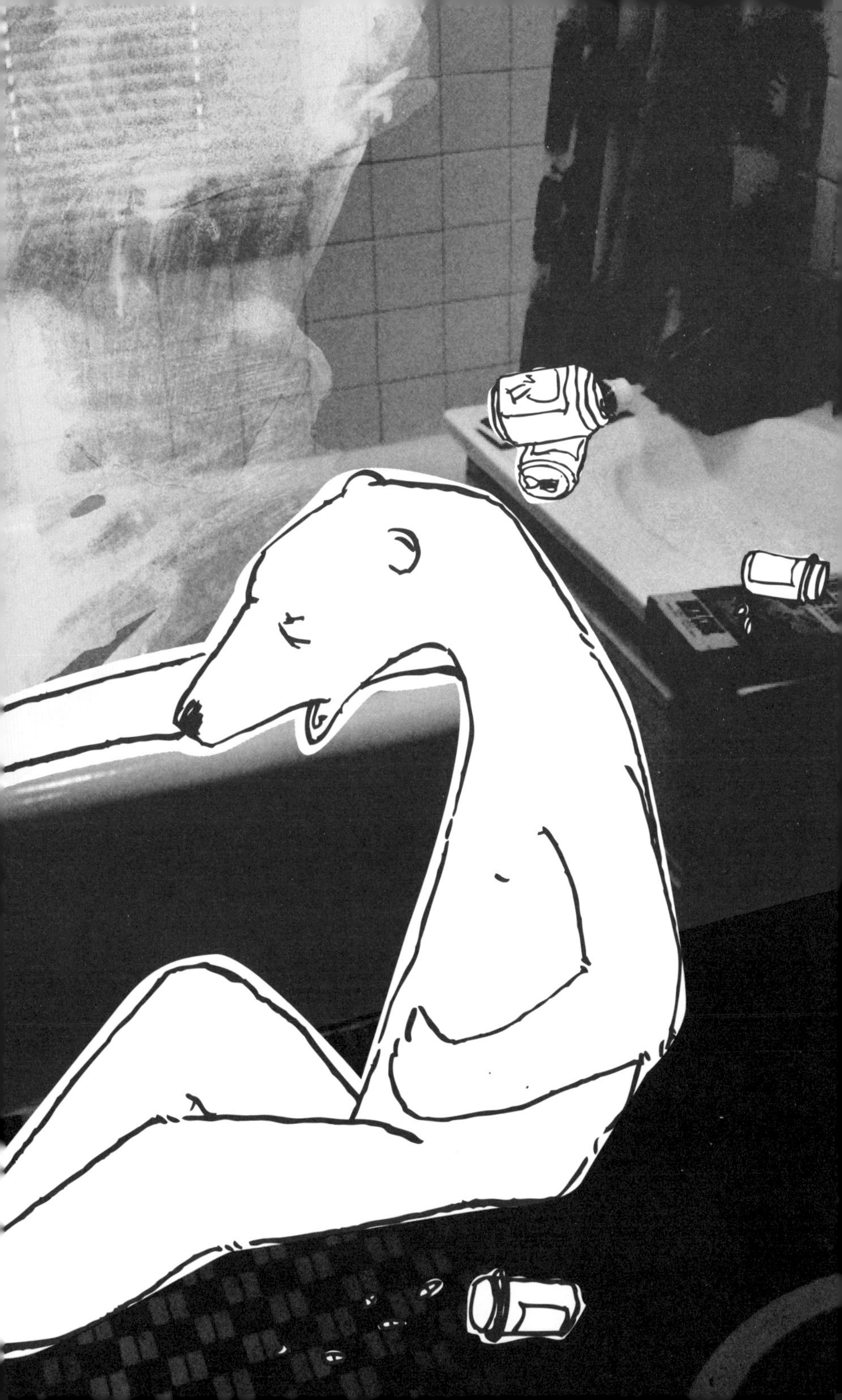

ing into the bathroom, "You were a fucking animal. *Genius*. Don't forget to leave your number on the kitchen table before you take off. But feel free to stay as long as you want."

My mouth was parched, eyes watering and goopy, head pounding, and beneath it all, churning like an invisible riptide, my heart was out of control, and I couldn't breathe properly. I heard a sing-songy "Bye," and the front door to the apartment slammed shut, and for a moment the air was completely still and quiet. But not my chest. I tried to inhale slowly and steadily, like I'd learned on set with the on-call Yoga instructor before shooting particularly challenging and potentially emotionally draining scenes. But nothing worked.

Darkness started to creep in on all sides, but before it did I noticed there were pills scattered all around me and stuck in my fur—black ones, red ones, yellow ones—so I grabbed a couple of the closest and gulped them down with water from the spigot, then sat back and waited. Soon I was gone. My nose pressed against the cool tile floor. I closed my eyes and wondered if my heart would ever beat regularly again. Or at all. It was an amusing thought, whether I died or lived, it was so simple. And honestly I could not care less either way.

XXII

I woke up later that evening when I heard the front door fling open and a optimistic "Anybody here?" from the guy whose apartment it was. I could scarcely pry my eyes open, but there he was blurrily hovering over me with a knowing, lascivious grin across his greasy face. "I'm so glad you stayed."

Flashes from the night before flooded me, and it took everything I had to bolt up and push past this guy, who was already loosening his tie in some sort of sick anticipation—of what, I'm still afraid to wonder, but I know it wasn't pretty.

"Where are you going?" he pleaded as he tailed me, but I was out the door, down the stairs, and on the sidewalk in mere seconds.

Stumbling across Tompkins Square Park I stepped up to the Temperance fountain and braced myself over it, splashing some cool water on my face. I watched the beads trickle off my fur into the stone basin. After a while a pack of rowdy, smelly gutter punks came up behind me and poked a bottle of malt liquor into my back. I turned around and took it, gulping half the liquid in the bottle before I realized it didn't taste right. I'm pretty certain it was urine from the way they laughed and coughed their TB coughs at me. I smashed the bottle on the ground by their feet, and the punks turned to go, still howling. But one of them hung back; he must've felt sorry for me and offered one of his clove cigarettes. And I wasn't too proud to take it.

I sat on a bench in the park smoking in the night breeze. It occurred to me vaguely like deja vu that I'd missed work again that day. My boss was probably going to give me my walking papers this time, because I'd already been given a couple stern warnings.

Another thing that suddenly occurred to me there on that bench: that I was a colossal failure and nothing more than blight on the face of the planet, a gaping hole in the ozone layer only making it worse for everybody else. In other words: rock bottom.

My boss at Mud was the one who first suggested I start attending meetings. He was in AA and saw a bit of his old self in me—he said he'd give me another chance if I cleaned up. But I couldn't just go occasionally or bullshit my way through. At first I figured, *Fuck him*, yes I can fake it, and that's precisely what I'm going to do. But after a few meetings, sitting there listening to other people's stories, I realized I was no different from anybody else. And mostly: that I had a major problem that wasn't going to go away on its own.

Alcoholics Anonymous, Narcotics Anonymous, and even Al-Anon—that holy trinity saved my life. I cut myself off from my toxic bear friends and lifestyle, found a different place to live where drug deals weren't transacting at all hours of the day. My entire existence became limited to work every day and meetings every night. I started gaining weight back, getting on a regular sleep schedule, feeding myself properly. And I started noticing things again—like a lady's whimsical pink hat on 2nd Avenue, or the way the afternoon sun catches the top-floor windows in the old synagogue across from my new apartment.

Fame, Kabbalah, Scientology, none of it could do a thing for me until I admitted my life was completely

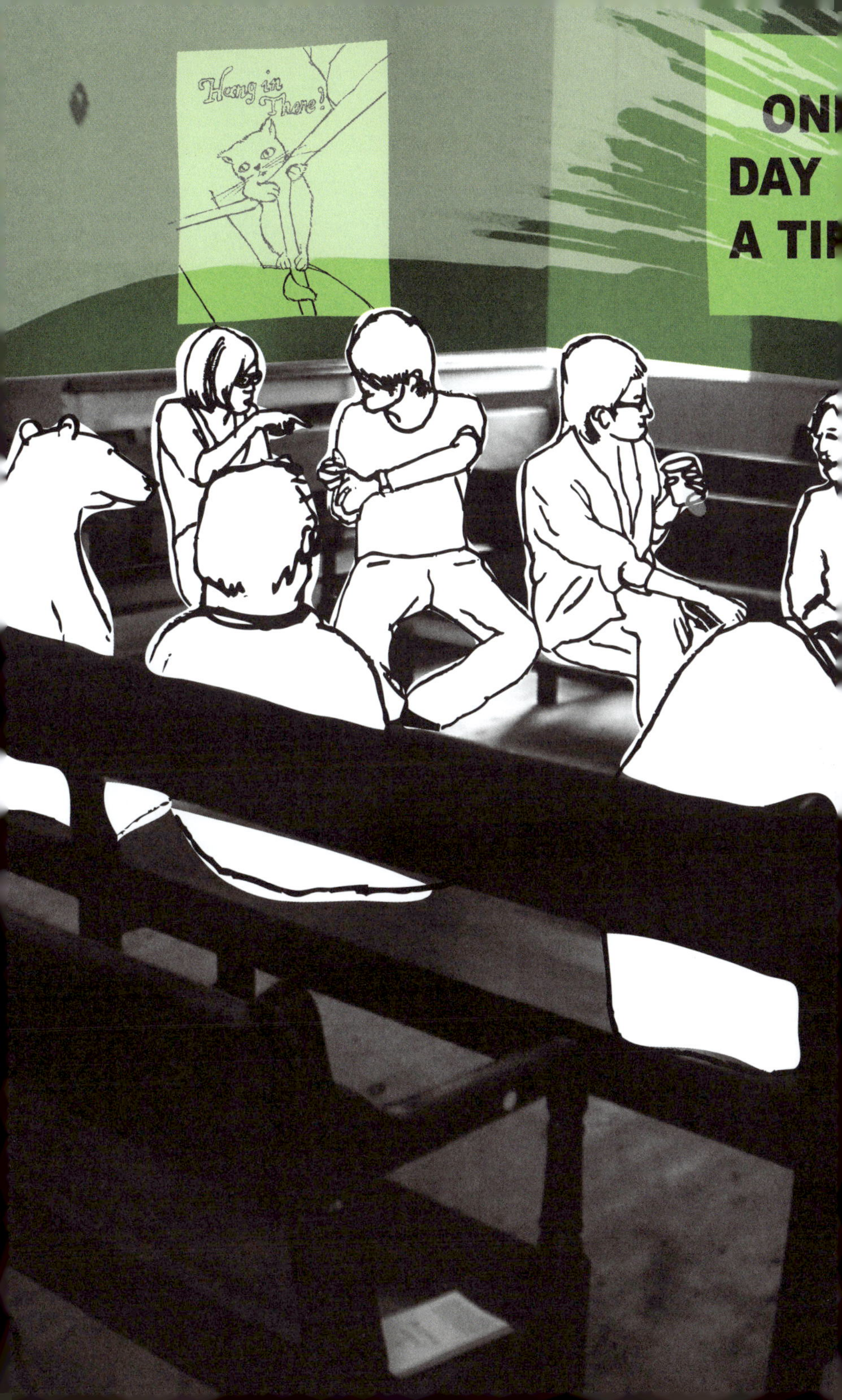
Hang in There!
ON
DAY
A TI

unmanageable. That I had a disease, and I needed help to recover from it.

My name is Beaufort, and I'm an alcoholic.
My name is Beaufort, and I'm an addict.
My name is Beaufort, and I am Al-Anonic.

At my home AA meeting in the basement of a Spanish-speaking church on St. Mark's Place, it was my pleasure to come early and set up chairs, spread out literature, and put out some coffee before the meetings. Service was part of my recovery, the concept of "doing the right thing for the right reason" something that had woefully become entirely foreign to me in the years since I'd left home. I realized that the concept was something my mother and father instilled in me, though I'd clearly forgotten that way of life. It was my sponsor Micah who helped me start forgiving my mother—for everything—and making amends to people I'd alienated along the way (Leo being first and foremost). Forgiving and being forgiven was the best feeling in the world—better than being high or smashed or numbed out in any of the myriad ways I'd grown accustomed to of late.

I didn't quite buy the whole "God" part, but I had devised my own understanding of a higher power, and was working my 12 Steps harder than I'd ever worked anything in my entire life. I was completely clean and sober. And doing my goddamnedest to accept the things I couldn't change, the courage to change the things I could, and the wisdom to know the difference.

XXIII

My boss at Mud promoted me to barista, first in the shop, and then on the Mud Truck in Astor Place. I was responsible for setting up the equipment each morning, managing the daily service while parked by the 6-train entrance all day, and then getting the truck back and breaking it down each night. It was a lot of responsibility, and I feared failing my boss again, but I loved what I did. I loved meeting people and being a tiny part of contributing to their days—even if it was in the form of a small iced Caffe Americano with a splash of simple syrup.

My recovery was going beautifully: I celebrated six months of sobriety with a medallion ceremony and a night of bowling with my sponsor Micah and a few other friends from the program. I think I was coming back to the real Beaufort again, or perhaps making his acquaintance for the very first time. I liked what I saw, and I wanted to see what else he might contribute to this world. I journaled a lot as part of the program, and I started noticing that my entries were growing more and more creative, with ideas for stories, or even little scenes from my life, piling up in the margins.

Micah was active in the downtown avant-garde theater community, and he didn't push, but when the time was right, he invited me to a show one night.

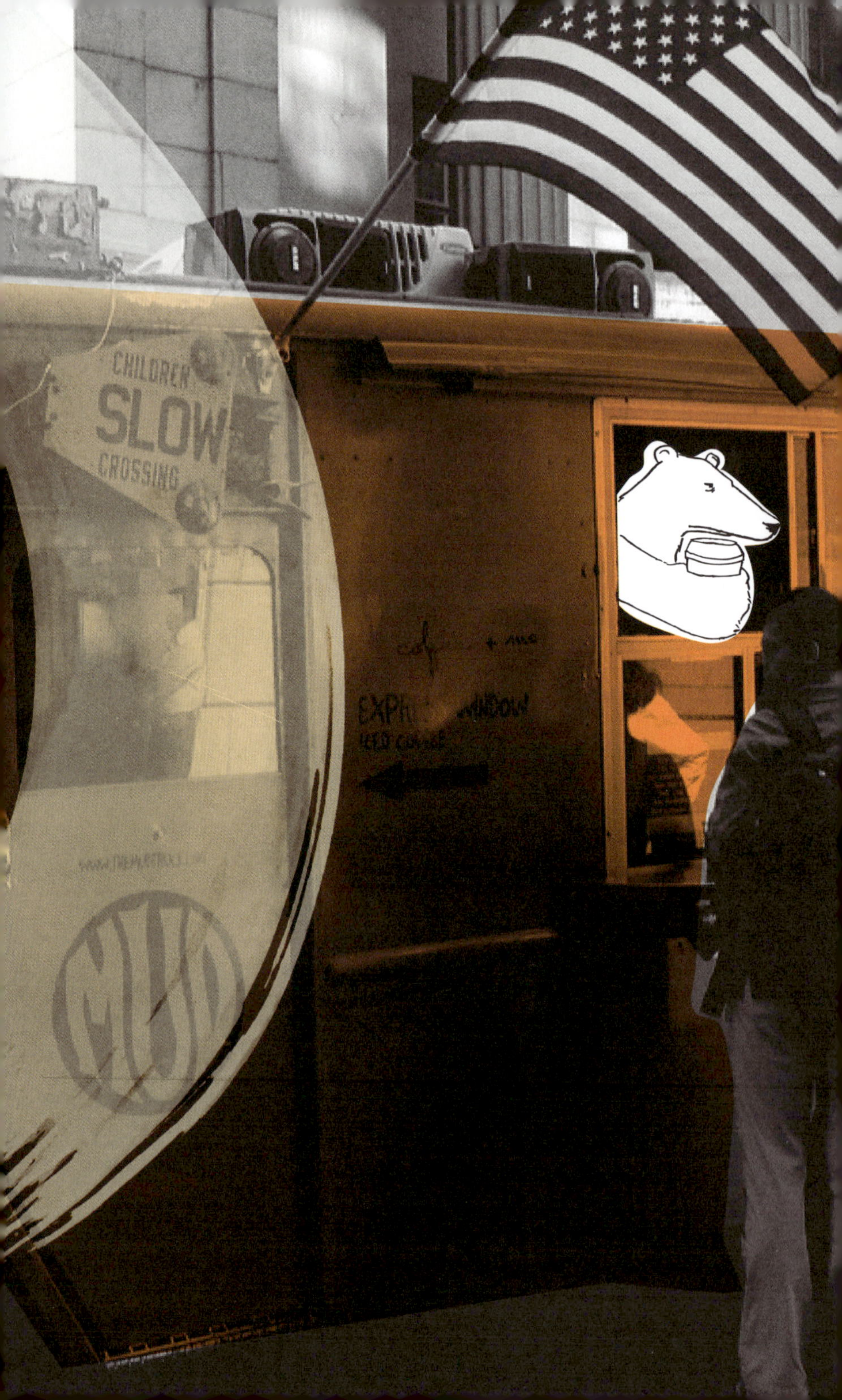
CHILDREN
SLOW
CROSSING

I was blown away by the energy, the overall quality of the work, and the collective process involved in the production—all for a couple dozen people in the audience. No opening weekend numbers, no competing with other releases and re-designing posters and marketing to capitalize on different aspects of the product in order to attract as many demographics as possible. It was *so* authentic.

Micah knew about *Bear*, knew I'd always hoped to tell my story. Knew also, acutely, how dreadfully wrong that endeavor turned out the first time around. He lent me plays and books to read (Spaulding Gray and Jim Carroll to name a couple), took me to shows (like Justin Bond's *Lustre: A Mid-Winter TransFest* at P.S. 122), and opened my eyes to a brave new world of storytelling combined with performance. I soon got involved doing stage managing of a show at the Loisaida Underground theater, and learned from the inside out what goes into collectively producing a show in the off-off Broadway theater world. It was more of an education than anything I'd learned in the film industry, and I was a newborn babe in the woods, soaking up any and everything.

And then suddenly, like some ladies say lightening strikes and they realize they have to become mothers, I realized I wanted to do a show of my own. Nothing too complicated. Just a simple one-man deal where I'd stand up there and be completely honest and myself for the first time in my life. Easy, right?

So I bought myself a used laptop from a depressive failed-novelist-turned-celebrity-stylist I found on Craigslist. And got to work writing my story.

XXIV

My life expanded slightly to accommodate working on the Mudtruck, attending AA meetings—and yes, writing my monologue. Every spare minute found me feverishly pawing my MacBook, telling the truths I'd always been afraid would prove the death of me if I ever completely revealed them. The process was entirely freeing, and not the kind of free I'd felt with Tina and the boys, or when I was writing *Bear*, posing at the Coffee Bean & Tea Leaf in Hollywood and incessantly nattering on with other poseurs who believed they were doing the work of god or some shit. This was flaying myself and turning my insides out for everybody to see. Only I didn't care if a million people or nobody saw it. This story was for me.

When the Loisaida Underground offered to produce my one-bear show, I wasn't entirely certain I wanted to do it. But Micah thought it would be a healthy process for me to see something through from start to finish, so after a few more rounds of edits, they assigned me a director, and we went into production. Just me on stage, seated at a wooden desk with a lamp, a mic, and a glass of ice water. Minimal spot-lighting. The story of my life. Not running from my past, but rather running straight into it. No more playing the global warming card.

Time Out New York and *The Village Voice* both ran promising previews, and tickets were selling at a decent clip as a result of the coverage. The theater added some more nights, making it a two-week run, and it was by about the third or fourth show, I believe, that we'd ironed out most of the kinks. So I was feeling bullish about my focus and preparation on the night that the director of the Fringe Festival appeared in the audience. Afterwards he came backstage and made a formal offer to include me in his upcoming festival. It was a huge opportunity to take it to the next level, though I'd have sincerely been happy if I'd ended up doing a one-night run for an audience composed solely of a few AA buddies and some seat-filling stragglers from the Delancey Street off-track-betting facility.

Finally, I was truly free from the prison of "What's next?" *One day at a time*, baby.

The weekend before closing night, a small piece about my show ran in *The New York Times* Arts section. It hinted at a "comeback," but more importantly suggested that my small tale was potentially capable of effecting some sort of change: "If this dispatch from one of the northernmost corners of the globe doesn't convince the U.S. to ratify the Kyoto Protocol, what will?"

People at the Loisaida were buzzing; it was the first time the *Times* had covered one of their shows. But on closing night I was more thrilled about the

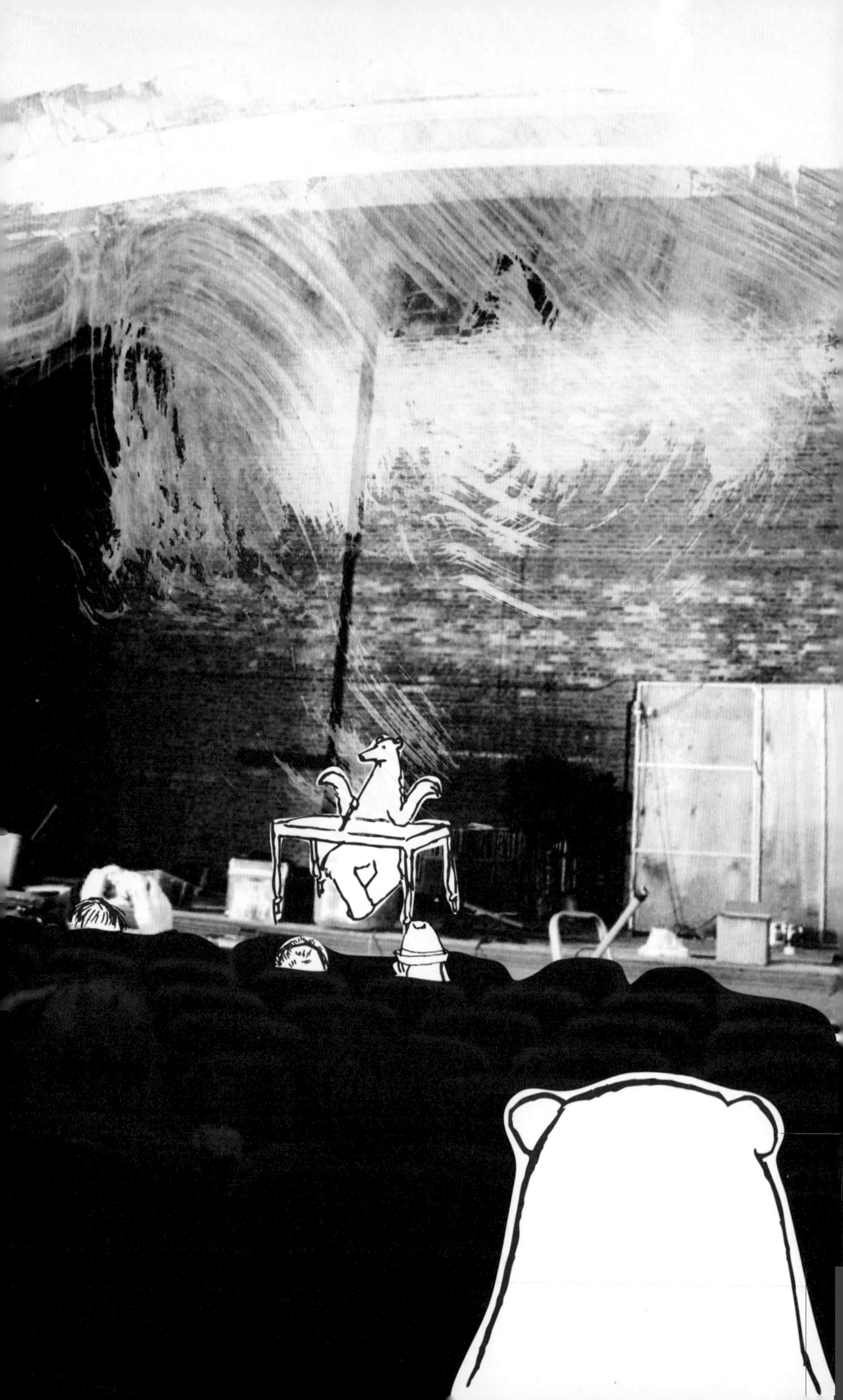

bunch of flowers that showed up at my dressing table. An envelope was attached, the card inside:

> *Break a Paw, Bro.*
> *—Leo*

It ended up being my best show of the whole run. About three-quarters of the way through, panting under the lights, I paused to take a drink of water, and a big ice cube accidentally slid into the back of my throat. I gagged a little, which took me out of the monologue for a few seconds. But I wasn't worried. While I was collecting myself, I spotted a shadowy figure up in the last row of the theater, and it felt very familiar, though in both the moment and the darkness, I couldn't quite make out who or what it was.

I took a few beats to further compose myself before delivering the final lines of the play, and then the words just started pouring out of me like a nightingale's song—I wasn't even conscious that I was delivering any lines. It was just me. When I put my head down on the table and the lights went dark, the audience stood and applauded.

After the wrap party, the theater emptied. Micah asked whether I felt like having company on the walk home, but I said I just wanted to be alone in the comfortingly crisp winter air. And when I stepped out the back door of the theater and into the alley, I thought I was alone. That is, until the figure from the last row appeared and placed a large warm paw on my shoulder. It was my father. He had a note. From my mother. She wanted me to know she'd only sent me away because she couldn't feed me anymore. Couldn't even feed herself. She drowned between ice floes the day after we separated; my father couldn't get back in time, and my mother figured I'd have a better chance surviving down South than with her. She felt like an embarrassment and a failure, unable to feed her only son. She left a note explaining all of this, and my father wanted me to have it. He'd been tracking me for years, and he could always tell there was something missing, something I needed to hear.

XXV

I knew the whole time I was telling this story that it was a cover for the real story, which for some reason I still find impossible to tell. So that's all I'm going to say. I should probably also tell you what happened after the Fringe Festival, when I went Off-Broadway and then toured a bunch of North American cities and Europe with the show. Or about the three-part BBC television special. But I don't really feel like it. And it's not what's most important now anyhow.

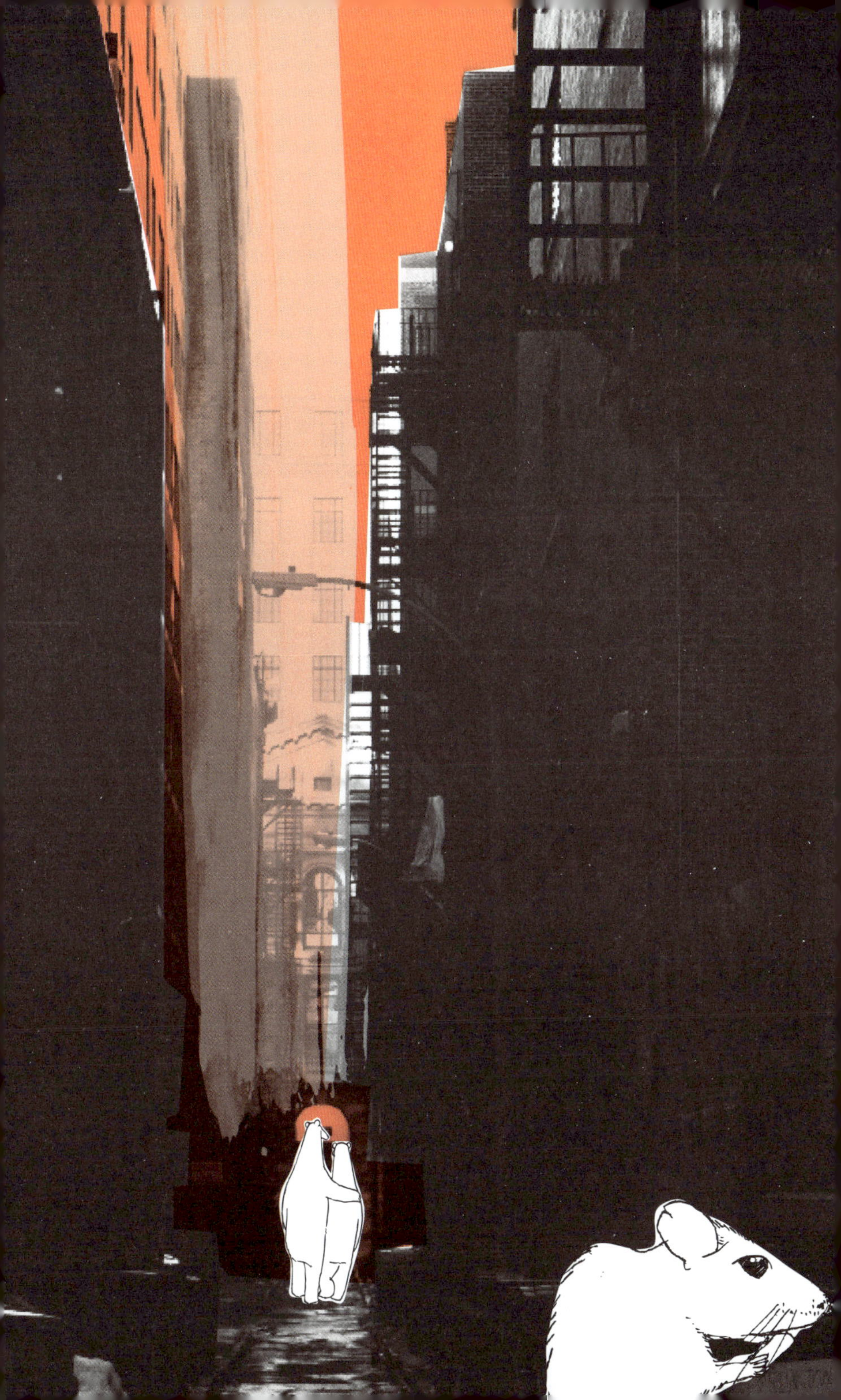

ACKNOWLEDGEMENTS

*The author is deeply grateful to
the following individuals and places:*

Dennis Loy Johnson, Valerie Merians, Daniel O'Connor, Megan Halpern and everybody at the excellent Melville House
Niko Hansen and Tim Jung at Arche/Atrium in Deutschland
Doug Stewart at Sterling Lord Literistic
Alex Petrowsky at himself
The Millay Colony for the Arts
Ledig House International

And to these people and creatures:

Diane Baldwin, Kate Bornstein, Maud Casey, Fredrica Cooper, Murray Cooper, Steve Cooper, Kimmie David, David Duchovny, Jeni Englander, Brigitte Jakobeit, Téa Leoni, Adam Mansbach, Milton, Mom & Dad, Rick Moody, Richard Nash, Mr. Slutherpants, Amanda Patten, Amy Ray, Rosie, Turner Schofield, Johnny Temple and James Withers (for knowing the Heimlich Maneuver).

And to my lovely and amazing wife Allison [Glock] Cooper, who is responsible for anything funny in this book.

T COOPER is the author of the novels *Lipshitz Six, or Two Angry Blondes*, and *Some of the Parts*, as well as co-editor of the anthology *A Fictional History of the United States With Huge Chunks Missing*. His work has appeared in a variety of publications and anthologies, including the *New Yorker*, the *New York Times*, and the *Believer*, among many others. Cooper lives in New York with his family.

ACKNOWLEDGEMENTS

*The author is deeply grateful to
the following individuals and places:*

Dennis Loy Johnson, Valerie Merians, Daniel O'Connor, Megan Halpern and everybody at the excellent Melville House
Niko Hansen and Tim Jung at Arche/Atrium in Deutschland
Doug Stewart at Sterling Lord Literistic
Alex Petrowsky at himself
The Millay Colony for the Arts
Ledig House International

And to these people and creatures:

Diane Baldwin, Kate Bornstein, Maud Casey, Fredrica Cooper, Murray Cooper, Steve Cooper, Kimmie David, David Duchovny, Jeni Englander, Brigitte Jakobeit, Téa Leoni, Adam Mansbach, Milton, Mom & Dad, Rick Moody, Richard Nash, Mr. Slutherpants, Amanda Patten, Amy Ray, Rosie, Turner Schofield, Johnny Temple and James Withers (for knowing the Heimlich Maneuver).

And to my lovely and amazing wife Allison [Glock] Cooper, who is responsible for anything funny in this book.